THE SPY KILLER

THE SPY KILLER

JIMMY SANGSTER

BRASH
BOOKS

ISBN: 1-941298-40-0
ISBN-13: 978-1-941298-40-4

Published by
Brash Books, LLC
12120 State Line #253,
Leawood, Kansas 66209
www.brash-books.com

PUBLISHER'S NOTE

This book was originally published in the United Kingdom in 1967 under the title *private I* and reflects the cultural and sexual attitudes, language, and politics of the period. ... as well as the punctuation and spelling.

To John Paddy Carstairs

PROLOGUE

THE slamming of the door sounded like the last crack of doom. It had an utter finality about it. If I ever heard another voice or saw another person, it would be a surprise. I might as well have been embalmed, placed in a coffin, and buried a hundred miles deep.

For one moment a disembodied eye peered through a hole in the door. Then that was withdrawn and a metal slide replaced it. And there I was, *finis, kaput, terminado*, the absolute and ultimate end.

The straitjacket I was wearing was not looped too tightly, and there's a trick for getting out of them. Unfortunately, nobody has ever taught me the trick, so I lay there with my arms wrapped round myself and tied at the back, like a dressed fowl ready for the oven. The only thing needed to complete the synonym was stuffing, and that had long since gone. It had been beaten, medicated, thumped, interrogated and brainwashed out of me.

I was now classified as an A-1, first class, top grade, number one type lunatic.

My medical dossier, two inches thick, had been stamped INCURABLE and was safely filed away.

The real crunch was that it was all so legal. The certifying doctors, three of them, were pillars of respectability, doyens of their profession. They had examined me minutely over a period of a month. Finally, jointly and severally, as the legal termination has it, they had reached their findings. The three of them had put their names to the certificate of insanity. The poor deluded buggers couldn't have done otherwise. As far as they were concerned, my symptoms were classic and genuine. There was no way they could know about the needles I'd had jabbed into my backside in the middle of the night, needles that ossified my brain, paralysed my nervous system, and turned me into a gibbering idiot for days at a stretch.

As far as they were concerned, Bruno was just another male nurse. Big Bruno, with a face that looked like a badly packed suitcase, and whose gentle brown eyes stayed gentle while he was pumping a patient full of Pheno this, Para that, and God knows what else. Or while he was using those great lumps he called hands, carefully feeling for the nerve centres where an ounce of pressure could deliver a ton of pain. I couldn't help but admire Bruno though, and the day I cut his throat with a blunt penknife, as I have privately sworn to do, I'm sure that I shall regret the passing of a true professional. Max should be proud of Bruno, the last of the Great Inquisitors, the pain maker, the creator of insanity. But then Max has always chosen his people carefully. I think the only mistake he ever made was me.

Of course, it would have been far simpler for him to have disposed of me in the time honoured manner. To give him credit, he'd tried. But fortunately for us both, he hadn't succeeded. Because stupid as I sometimes am, I'm not so stupid that I don't take certain precautions along the line. Now, my life insurance policies rest secure in two safety deposit boxes, while as an added precaution my bank manager holds certain documents, about the contents of which he knows nothing. All that he does know is that I'm now locked up in a lunatic asylum, and somehow or other he's going to have to explain away my overdraft to head office.

Had Max disposed of me in the normal way, the documents would have been forwarded circuitously to the faceless gentlemen who spend their lives in anonymity and wield their power with awesome indifference. Max, Bruno, Danielle, all of them would have disappeared quietly, without a ripple to mark their passing. At least that way I would have had the satisfaction of not going down alone.

It's getting late now. I wonder if Bruno will keep on with the injections now that their purpose has been accomplished. The doctors have all returned to their staid and lucrative practices, there's no longer anyone to whom it is necessary for me to exhibit my lunatic tendencies.

That in itself is a relief. The slipping away of sanity which followed the injection was something to be experienced. One tiny corner of the mind would stand back objectively and watch the remainder dissolve into chaos. And soon even that small core would give way before the onslaught. What followed I never knew. I only know that hours later, when sanity began to return, the same way as it departed, that tiny eye in the mind opened on to things that both horrified and revolted.

Fingernails torn from scratching at the walls, a bleeding scar on the wrist where I had bitten myself; blood, vomit, excrement, and a thin wailing, blubbering gibberish, issuing from a mouth over which at first the mind had no control. This was the evidence of what had gone before. What that was, I have no desire to know. I have never been proud of my body. Unlike some people, it has always been to me a machine that functions well or indifferently, depending on how much work you ask it to do, and how much care and time you are willing to spend on maintenance. I know that I am nearly two stone overweight, that my digestive system plays up constantly, that my teeth aren't particularly good, and that I have suffered periodically from halitosis, B.O., prickly heat and dandruff. But then I have never been particularly ashamed of my body either, not until those moments when I groped my way out of God knows what, and looked upon this battered, stinking, filthy carcass, and shuddered at what I must have turned into under the aegis of Bruno's needle.

There's no doubt that Max could have put me into a permanent state of insanity. A few extra c.c.s of whatever it was that Bruno used, and I would have slipped far enough over the edge, never to return.

But Max wouldn't do that. If I were truly insane, then I would no longer be aware of my predicament. And awareness was part of the scheme of things. This was Max's way of saying "You've been a bad boy and now you must suffer the consequences." He's a vindictive bastard, and must derive great satisfaction from the knowledge that I could be suffering my punishment for the rest of my life. A bullet or a knife would have been quicker, but the true essence would have been missing. And anyway, there were the insurance policies.

So Max had given me four, blank anonymous walls to live with, and perhaps if I'm a good boy, in a couple of years they'll let me spend an hour a day with the real lunatics who are now my compatriots.

I've seen some of them during my periodic trips along the corridors. They have the vacant stare, the slack mouth, the crafty crazed expression of true madness. They cringe, they whimper, they strut and they shout. There are schizophrenics, paranoiacs, psychopaths; there's every damn shade of lunacy with one common denominator, they're all highly dangerous. They're dangerous both to themselves and to anyone misguided enough to turn their backs for half a second. This isn't one of those "open wall" institutions where the inmates are allowed into the town, there to embarrass the populace. Here, the walls are twelve feet high, the doors are steel, and the beds bolted to the floor. Here, if a man isn't in a straitjacket at least once a week, he's a cissy. This is the place where the male nurses are six feet tall and carry leather covered coshes in their hip pockets.

They strap you to the table to shave you; all food is liquid so there can be no need for cutlery (even a spoon can be broken and used as a gouge). There's no glass, no wire, no fitments, no belts, suspenders or neckties. We wear long cotton shifts, reinforced in the weaving so that they cannot be torn into strips. That is when we wear anything at all; most of the time we're kept stark naked. Our fingernails are kept trimmed very low. Our hair is cut very short. I've a strong suspicion that after a couple of weeks, they pull all your teeth as well, just to be one hundred per cent sure.

Now it seems I have nothing to do for the next thirty-odd years except to think about Max, and about the stupid, idiotic, bloody fool way I managed to get myself into this.

CHAPTER ONE

IT was a Monday, a wet, miserable Monday. I'd spent the weekend following the over-sexed wife of a client and making copious notes. She had fallen in and out of so many beds in the course of forty-eight hours, that I had begun to doubt even my own count. My client had asked for evidence, what I'd got for him was a revelation. The only surprising thing was his wanting a divorce at all. It was a wonder she hadn't killed him from exhaustion years ago.

The weekend, too, had been wet. My shoes had started to leak and I had been unable to find time to get home and change them. I had managed about six hours' sleep, all in the car. I had eaten stale sandwiches and doubtful meat pies, and those only when I could escape long enough from my subject's amatory gymnastics to find a cafe.

I had finally reached home at four o'clock that morning, and now, tired and extremely irritable, I was on the way to the office to type up the notes. They had to be made to sound lurid in the legal sense rather than the erotic.

I was rolling a phrase around my tongue, something like "the subject was observed momentarily at a first-floor window in a state of undress," when I emerged from the Piccadilly Underground to find that it was still raining.

I debated for a moment whether I'd stop at the Corner House for some breakfast. Then I decided that I would treat myself to lunch instead. In my constant battle with overweight, it was always breakfast *or* lunch. I crossed Shaftesbury Avenue and was walking past Cecil Gee's before I was aware of it. The overcoat was still in the window. One hundred per cent cashmere, sixty-five guineas. I tortured myself daily by looking at it.

"One day," I said to myself. "One day."

As usual, the dustbin on the stairs hadn't been emptied, and as usual on a Monday morning, somebody had used the letter box facing into Old Compton Street as a toilet some time during the weekend. So, the passage stank, and the stairs stank and, when I reached the outer office, that stank too. When it rained Miss Roberts' cheap fur coat smelled like a stable that needs mucking out. She smiled at me as I came in.

"Good morning, Mr. Smith," she said brightly. My name really is Smith, and to make it doubly distinguished my parents christened me John. "We are early this morning."

Miss Roberts was about thirty-five and looked fifty. She was a kindly, inefficient body, who seemed to have come with the lease. I shared the premises with a man named Stubbs. We each had our own room leading from the outer office, and Miss Roberts provided the only link between us. She answered the phone, took messages and made the tea. She would tell me everything about Stubbs, and no doubt told him everything about me. Stubbs ran an abortive theatrical agency, and I ran an abortive enquiry agency. Between us, we aborted together, always behind in the rent, the rates, the telephone, and Miss Roberts' salary.

She continued to smile as I crossed towards my own office. I was about to go in when she delivered her news.

"*You* have an appointment," she said.

"I have?" I said.

"Eleven o'clock, a Mrs. Dunning. She phoned."

I thanked her and walked through into my office, leaving her rattling the tea cups. The mail was on my desk, two bills, a circular, and a message in Miss Roberts' spidery hand. Mrs. Dunning. Eleven p.m. I had once spent an hour trying to explain to Miss Roberts the difference between a.m. and p.m.

I hung up my raincoat and took my weekend notes from the pocket. I spread them on the desk and spent the next five minutes sorting them out. During this time Miss Roberts arrived with the first of an endless supply of cups of weak tea. She would keep the tea coming just as long as there was anyone in the office. The fact that one could only swallow so much tea in the course of a day didn't bother her. She would remove the untouched cup, which was now cold, shake her head, and place a fresh cup of the same brew in its place.

However, this was the first of the morning, and I drank it while I reread the notes. Then I pulled the typewriter towards me and started work.

At ten forty-five I had finished. I sorted them, stapled them together, and put them in a neat pile at the side of the desk. My client would be calling for them that afternoon, and was he in for a shock. Then, with nothing to do for the next fifteen minutes, I took stock. This is something I do periodically, an exercise that never fails to depress me. It involves thumbing back through my cheque book, wondering where the hell all the money has gone to. The fact that there is very little money to go *anywhere* makes the task easier. Then come some rapid calculations on the back of an envelope which confirm what I already know, namely that I am spending money at roughly twice the rate I am earning it. As always, this masochistic exercise in personal finance ended by my tearing up the envelope and slamming my cheque book into the drawer. And at this point Miss Roberts announced Mrs. Dunning.

I suppose I should have remembered. Somewhere, somehow, I had heard that Danielle had married a man named Dunning. But that was three years ago, and unimportant information doesn't stick. She looked marvelous, of course. She was one of those flowers that bloom in the warm glow of money, and obviously Mr. Dunning supplied plenty of that. She was wearing a soft suede coat with mink collar and lapels. Her handbag and shoes alone must have cost as much as I earned in three months.

Her face was carefully made up so that it looked as though she wasn't wearing any make-up at all, and as always, her hair was impeccable, red now where it had been blonde.

She smiled as she came in.

"Darling!" she said.

I saw Miss Roberts' expression as she closed the door behind Danielle. What a tidbit for Stubbs *that* would make.

Danielle held out her cheek for me to peck at, and her involuntary withdrawal as I did so was almost well enough concealed for me not to notice it.

Then she sat down, arranging herself tidily on my only visitor's chair, and crossing her legs demurely.

"You've put on weight," she said.

"So have you." She had, too, only on her it looked good.

'We're older, John," she said.

"A hundred years older," I said, sitting down at my desk.

"You haven't had your teeth fixed yet." She still had the faculty for bringing out into the open the thing which you most wanted ignored.

"I can't afford it," I said.

"Poor John. Business not too good?" She allowed her eyes to flick briefly round the room. "What a very brown room."

It was. It's the *brownest* room I've ever seen. The walls are brown, the floor and ceiling are brown. Not a rich, warm brown, but a dirty beige-type brown that overwhelms with depression so that even the green filing cabinet seems brown.

She looked back at me.

"You're losing your hair, too," she said. The whole conversation needed re-routing before she started to ask whether my sexual prowess had continued to deteriorate along with the rest of me. I knew that she would, too, if I didn't force her to change direction. I should have asked her how she was, or commented on how well she looked, or enquired whether she had been happy since she divorced me. But I didn't.

"What do you want, Danielle?" I asked.

Her eyebrows lifted a fraction.

"To see you," she said finally. I shook my head. She looked at me for a moment, then she lowered her eyes.

"No," she agreed. "I need your help."

Before I could say anything, she continued.

"Professionally, of course," she said. "I want to engage your services."

"What as?" I asked.

She waved her hand.

"This," she said, embracing the office. "John Smith, enquiry agent."

"*Mr.* Dunning?" I said.

She pouted. It was a "little girl" expression which had never suited her.

"I'm afraid so," she said.

I felt easier. Now I was on familiar ground. I dragged a pad towards me and took out a pen.

"Name, address and details of what you want me to do," I said a little pompously.

"Nathaniel Dunning, fourteen A, Eggerton Crescent, South West One."

I wrote it down and waited. When nothing else was said, I looked up.

"Well?" I asked.

"I thought *you* would tell me," she said. "That's why I came."

"Do you want him followed?" I asked.

"That's it," she said. "I want him followed."

"You have reason to believe he is conducting an extramarital relationship," I prompted.

She looked at me for a moment, then she burst out laughing. She threw her head back, exposing her long, fine neck. It was one of her better features, and she had learned to use it. I waited until she had finished laughing. I didn't even smile.

"I'm sorry, John," she said eventually. She stopped laughing with an effort. "Yes, I have reason to believe he is conducting an extramarital relationship." Her eyes still laughed.

"And you wish me to obtain evidence to this fact that will be of use in a court of law?" I said.

"Yes, I wish you to obtain evidence to ..."

"Tell me about it," I cut in, realising I was losing the initiative.

Quite suddenly her eyes and mouth went hard.

"The bastard's having it off somewhere, and I want to know all about it," she said.

This took me by surprise. She had only used vulgar speech, as she called it, when we were in bed together. Outside those unguarded moments she had spared no effort to let me know that she disapproved of it strongly. Some of my surprise must have showed.

"I've shocked you," she said.

"Not shocked," I said. "Surprised."

"I'm different, John. That bastard has changed me. Boy, how he's changed me."

I refrained from saying he deserved congratulations. Any man who had managed to change Danielle for better or for worse must have had something going for him. During the five years we had spent together, she had been as unchangeable as time itself.

"Have you any suspicions?" I asked, dragging it back to the professional once more.

"I *know*," she said. "Suspicions don't come into it."

"Then why do you need me?" I asked.

"I want it all legal, proved and notarised or whatever. I want it so that it will stand up in court."

"All right," I said. "Name of co-respondent?"

"Peter Alworthy."

I looked up.

"That's right," she said. "My husband's a queer. And if you laugh, I'll hit you over the head with that ashtray."

I had no intention of laughing. The whole thing had a poetic justice that was almost sublime. She saw it too, although she would never admit that her relationship with Marianne Pleshet had ever been more than that of a very good friend. The night I accused her of being a lesbian, she had hit me with a flower vase, packed a bag, and moved in—with Marianne. The subsequent divorce was provided by me. When I heard of her six months later, I realised that her lapse into lesbianism had been experimental and only temporary. But the affair with Marianne had not been the sole cause of my divorce, rather had it been the straw that broke this particular camel's back. And now, here she was, attempting to gather evidence for another divorce because her husband was a queer. It wasn't a laughing matter, but it was bloody amusing nevertheless.

"Well," she said, "don't you want to hear more?" I dragged myself back and tried to look professional again.

"Go on," I said.

"Peter Alworthy is a little fag who pretends to be a fashion photographer," she said.

"Pretends?"

"He takes dirty pictures as a side line. Nat sees him three times a week. He may see him more, I don't know."

"Perhaps your husband just likes dirty pictures," I said.

"*Queer* dirty pictures?"

"It's been known."

"He hasn't slept with me for over six months. If I touch him, he jumps a mile, and he insists on having his own bedroom."

"Have you tried to…" For some reason I felt embarrassed. Confessions are never easy, and for Danielle they had used to be downright impossible. But I wasn't her husband any more, I was a disinterested third party.

"I've tried everything," she said. "Barring rape. I'd try that if it wasn't a physical impossibility."

She *had* changed, and suddenly I wanted to get her off the hook.

I took down the name and address of Peter Alworthy and a couple more notes. Then we came to the crunch.

"This may take some time," I said.

"I don't care," she said.

"I *am* rather busy at the moment," I said. She saw what I was getting at.

"Dear John," she said. "You don't think I'd ask you to do this for nothing."

I had thought so, but I wasn't going to let her know.

"What is your normal fee?" she asked.

I added up quickly the amount of money I immediately owed and then added twenty-five per cent. I divided this by the number of days I thought I could stretch the affair.

"Fifteen pounds a day and expenses," I said, trying not to sound too hopeful.

"Do you mind cash?" she said, already delving into her handbag.

"Make it a hundred and fifty," I said. "If I can wrap it up in less than ten days, I'll refund the balance."

She pulled a roll of tenners from her handbag and started to count them off. The sight of all that money was so upsetting that I wanted to look away. I glanced at my notes.

"Where does your husband work?" I said.

She pushed fifteen ten pound notes towards me.

"He's something to do with the Foreign Office," she said.

If I hadn't been watching the money like a hypnotised rabbit, alarm bells might have started to sound there and then. As it was, I was too bloody greedy to see further than the sudden ability to pay the rent and eat well for the next three or four weeks.

I scooped the money towards me and casually slipped it into the desk drawer as though it was something I did every day.

"Have you got a photograph?" I asked, not very hopefully.

"No," she said. "Does it matter?"

I said that it didn't and took down the address of her husband's place of work. Then, because I could think of nothing else to say or do, I got to my feet to signify the end of the interview.

"Will you have dinner with me one night?" she said as I walked her to the door.

"Why?" I asked.

She shrugged.

"Talk about old times," she said.

The 'old times' she referred to seemed, in retrospect, to have been one continuous battle. There didn't seem much point in raking it over.

"Perhaps we should leave it until I've finished this job for you."

She looked at me as I opened the door to the outer office. Then she smiled and nodded.

"If you say so, dear," she said.

She reached up and kissed me on the mouth. Before I could react, she had gone, leaving me standing.

Miss Roberts closed the outer door behind her and looked at me with a new respect in her eyes.

"Ooh, Mr. Smith," she said.

Before she could enlarge on it, I reached for my raincoat, took the money from the drawer, and went to lunch.

With one hundred and fifty pounds in my pocket, it had to be Wheeler's in Old Compton Street. There was a bit of bother getting a table, but finally one was found for me on the third floor. It was practically in the kitchen, but who cared.

I ordered two dozen oysters, a sole *meunière,* and a bottle of Chablis. Then as I pigged it, surrounded by the noisy lunchtime crowd of film and near-film people, I took stock again.

Not financial stock this time. That had been temporarily taken care of. I took stock of Danielle and me, and the five years that had passed since I had left Danielle and the Service. I always linked the two, because I quit them both at the same time, although in fact they had little to do with one another. Perhaps when I decided to break with the Service, I had subconsciously wanted to make the break absolute, turning my back not only on my old professional life, but on my old social life as well. Both had been equally unrewarding, if not downright impossible. The marriage had been conceived in deceit and born into distrust. It had taken approximately two months for us both to realise that we had made a horrendous mistake. We were unsuited physically and psychologically. But having recognised this fact, we allowed the whole thing to drag on for three years before either of us could stir up enough enthusiasm to do anything about it. In actual fact it was on the night I quit the Service that I had accused Danielle of being a lesbian. So I suppose the incidents *were* connected, even if it was only by a disgruntled state of mind.

She was as relieved as I was to have found the catalyst which allowed us to go our own ways. As for my break with the Service, the less said about that the better.

By the time I had finished lunch, it was two forty-five and I was pleasantly drunk. I paid the bill, overtipped, and walked round to the bank two minutes before it closed. I paid in one hundred pounds of Danielle's money, keeping the balance for running expenses. Then I went back to the office.

At half past three, my client called for the weekend report on his wife. I watched his face while he read it through. There were tears in his eyes when he finished reading. He managed to blink them back like the man that he wasn't.

"Will this be sufficient for me to get a divorce?" he asked.

I felt like saying that it was sufficient to get his wife deported if he wanted, but I didn't. He thanked me as though I had done him a big favour, and settled his account. He obtained a promise from me that I would appear in court if necessary, for a fee of course, and he left.

Two pay days in six hours! Business was looking up. If things carried on like this for much longer, I'd be able to buy that cashmere coat *and* keep that long-standing appointment with my dentist to have my teeth capped. Miss Roberts then fed me endless cups of tea until I left at five o'clock.

A hundred yards from my office in Old Compton Street is a shop that sells overalls, jackets for waiters and other such gear. A beige dust coat set me back forty shillings. In a smelly passage nearby I unwrapped the parcel. Using my pen-knife I drilled three small holes into the lapels. Left and right. Where official messengers should wear their Crown-badges. Often they don't because they can't be bothered to change over when they send one coat to the laundry and put on a different one.

It had stopped raining and I walked down through Leicester Square and Trafalgar Square, and into Whitehall.

I called in at a stationer's on the way and bought a blue cardboard file, and half a ream of copy paper. I told the assistant not to wrap either. I put the paper into the file, giving it a nice bulky look. Before I left the shop, I wrote across the top of the file CODE E.2.

The address Danielle had given me fitted her description of her husband being "something to do with the Foreign Office," the building itself being exactly that.

In the street outside the main doors, I took off my raincoat and hung it carefully over the railings. I put on the dust-coat. With the file clutched under my arm, I pushed the door open and walked in. I hurried across to the sergeant's desk.

"Has the Principal Under-Secretary gone yet?" I said urgently.

The sergeant didn't even blink.

"He's still upstairs."

Without thanking him, because my business was far too urgent, I ran up the main stairs two at a time and turned left at the top. Once out of sight of the sergeant, I slowed down and tried to stop puffing and blowing. Any staircase taken two at a time leaves me like that these days.

I chose the third door on the right, Room 43. I knocked and went in.

A tall, dried-up looking man was just putting on his over-coat. He looked at me as I came in.

"Here's the file, sir," I said.

"What file?"

"Mr. Dunning, Room forty-three," I said.

"No Dunning here," he said, reaching for his umbrella.

"This *is* room forty-three," I said.

"That may be," he said. "But no Dunning. This is my office and my name's Ryman. Now if you'll excuse me..." he started towards the door.

"I'll leave it here anyway," I said, moving over to put it on the corner of his desk.

I saw him looking at it, its size and the cryptic classification on the cover. Whatever it was, he didn't want to be landed with it. Files meant work, and misdirected files meant even more work.

"Hang on," he said. He picked up a phone.

"Dunning, what's his room number?" he said. Then he nodded.

"Thank you." He hung up and turned to me.

"Dunning's in room one-two-seven, second floor. Take it up to him, there's a good chap."

I hesitated a moment, just long enough, then I nodded disagreeably.

"They said room forty-three," I grumbled, heading for the door.

"They also said Dunning. He's in room one-two-seven," he said.

He came out of the office behind me, smiled bleakly, and moved off towards the stairs.

I found room 127 at the end of the corridor on the second floor. I tapped on the door and walked in. Dunning was sitting at his desk working on some papers. He looked up as I came in. He had a certain flashy dignity about him, and I could see what might have originally impressed Danielle. Thin, well-drawn face, small military type moustache, and very pale blue eyes which could have been intimidating but weren't because of a nervous tick which caused him to blink his eyelids about five times more than normal. He *could* have been a queer, I suppose, but these days who the hell could ever tell. He looked at me enquiringly, his eyelids batting up and down like a semaphore.

"Mr. Ryman, sir?" I said.

"No," he said.

"This is room one-two-seven, isn't it?"

"Yes, it is. I'm Dunning."

I looked disappointed.

"Sorry, sir," I said. "Someone's given me the wrong room number."

He reached for the phone.

"I'll find out for you. Ryman, you said?"

"It doesn't matter," I said quickly. But he had already picked up the phone. I stood there looking humbly grateful while he ascertained that Ryman was in room forty-three. Then I thanked him and left.

I dropped the file in a wastebasket on my way down. The sergeant didn't even look up as I crossed the main hall, and walked out into Whitehall.

My raincoat was still on the railings where I had left it, which didn't say much for my raincoat. I put it on and crossed the road to a line of telephone booths. One was empty. I stepped in and closed the door behind me. Then I dialed the speaking clock.

"At the third stroke it will be five fifty-seven and forty seconds."

"Oh really," I said for the benefit of a man who was glaring into the phone booth, waiting to make a call. Then a booth was vacated somewhere along the line, and he disappeared.

It was quite easy to see the main entrance from where I was, and for the first ten minutes I watched a procession of men and women pour out, with no sign of Dunning. Periodically I disconnected the phone and dialed something else. I allowed my own home number to ring for five minutes; I dialed 999 and reported a multiple rape in Eaton Square; and I dialed TIME again and had spirited conversation with the recorded voice at the other end; and still no Dunning.

The flood of people leaving the building had now dwindled to a trickle, and something else had started to worry me. The combination of a bottle of Chablis and nine cups of tea was putting a serious strain on my bladder, and I knew that inside five minutes I would have to do something about it.

The five minutes passed. I said good-bye to the voice at the other end of the phone, and came out of the booth. There was a public toilet in Trafalgar Square, but that was four minutes' walk. Even if I could make it, I stood a very good chance of losing Dunning. So I lose him, I thought, I'll pick him up tomorrow. I started to hobble off in the direction of Trafalgar Square, and at that moment the inconsiderate bastard appeared.

He stood for a moment at the top of the steps, pulling on his gloves. Then he came down to street level and started to walk in the opposite direction to the one I had been going to take.

So I followed him, staying on the opposite side of the road, and moving like a man of a hundred and four.

He came into Parliament Square, and turned across it towards Broad Sanctuary. I could wait no longer. I raced down the steps of the Underground, spent an excruciatingly pleasant minute in the toilet, and raced up the steps again. I crossed the square at a run and headed down Broad Sanctuary. He hadn't let me down, he was there, five hundred yards in front of me. I walked fast until the gap had been narrowed to a hundred yards, where I stuck.

He turned into a pub in Petty France. He went to the saloon bar, so I went into the public. I ordered a large vodka, and before I could drink it, I saw him served with a bottle of wine and walk out again. Having paid for the vodka, I swallowed it much too quickly, and reached the street choking. He was fifty yards away. I staggered after him, and when he turned into the house, I was twenty-five yards behind him. He let himself in with his own key, and by the time I was level with the door, he had gone in and closed it behind him.

I walked on past the house to the end of the short street, and after a respectable pause, I walked back again.

The address was the one that Danielle had given me for Peter Alworthy, and I began to think that perhaps Danielle was on the right track.

Dunning had his own key for a start, and secondly the house *looked* as though it belonged to a queer. It was similar to its companions in the street, but it had been fussed over. Pink front door, twee coaching lamps and pretty little window boxes fully of pretty little flowers. The house itself looked like an age-ing queen.

I reached the end of the street once again and planned strategy. The bottle of wine pointed to the fact that they were going to dine. I could visualise the whole scene, candles stuck in old chianti bottles, Alworthy making like the little woman in the kitchen and serving *ratatouille*. There would be Ella Fitzgerald on the record player and pictures of guardsmen around the walls. I decided to allow them two hours to eat. Then I would try to get a closer look. Perhaps if things worked out, I'd come back tomorrow with a camera. One photograph was worth a dozen pages of typescript.

I walked back to the pub and this time went into the saloon bar. I ordered a plate of cold meat and potato salad, and a large vodka. I bummed an evening paper from the bartender and tucked myself in a corner to wait it out in comfort.

The bar was pleasantly busy, and after the third vodka I began to feel positively benevolent. A pretty girl in a short skirt was sitting up at the bar, and she occupied my attention for half an hour. I looked at her legs and indulged in lewd flights of fancy.

When she eventually left, I felt like I had been jilted. I considered whether or not to call Mary to fix up something for later that evening. I had been having an affair on and off with Mary for three years now, and bloody lucky I was too. She was a slim, sexy blonde of twenty-seven or thereabouts who modelled in a whole-sale dress house. She was not married, but had an understanding with her boss, who was. Saddled with a wife and four children he was forced to play it very cool indeed, and this allowed Mary plenty of free evenings. She was a good-hearted girl who also played it cool for the benefit of her boss who was besotted with her. So on the evenings she didn't see him, she usually stayed home. He had a sneaky habit of phoning her late at night when he was walking the dog, and if she wasn't in, there'd be hell to pay the following day. I'd suggested once to her that it wasn't a very ideal arrangement, and she should consider turning the whole thing in. But she liked her job, she was well paid, and she felt sorry for the poor bastard with his four kids, his dog and his wife who understood him only too well. I had nothing to offer her in exchange, so while not exactly telling me to mind my own business, that's what she implied.

Once or twice a week, whenever the fancy took me, I would call her and we would go out to dinner, or she would cook some-thing in her flat. Bed didn't always follow, but it followed often enough. I'm not very good in bed, but Mary never complained. Unlike Danielle, who had on occasions been known to complain loud and long. This is an area where even if a man knows he's no Casanova, he doesn't like to be reminded of it all the time. In fact, part of the trouble with Danielle had been due to her snide attacks on my virility, which decreased, as far as she was concerned, in a direct ratio to the amount of scorn she poured on it. It had become a descending spiral where the outcome had been that not only did I not want to sleep with her, but on the odd occasions that I tried, I only managed to confirm what she was saying.

Mary, however, never mentioned it, and I was, after three years, beginning to think that perhaps I wasn't such a limp handshake in bed as Danielle had led me to believe.

I looked at the clock on the wall of the bar. If I stayed there another half an hour, and then allowed an hour to prowl around the outside of Alworthy's house, I could be free by half past ten. I used the pub phone to call Mary. She answered a little breathlessly.

"Alone?" I asked. This was the standard opening gambit. My relationship with her was far too tenuous for me to want to queer anything good she might have had going. She always knew who it was.

"Hello, darling," she said. "What are you doing?"

"After half past ten, nothing," I said.

"Will you have eaten?" she asked.

I told her that I would have eaten and she said that she'd see me later. I returned to my drink feeling at peace with the world. I had a ten-day job that I'd probably wrap up in two, a medium-sized alcoholic glow, and a warm bed waiting for me.

During the last half an hour, I managed to find room for three more large vodkas. Then, bidding the barman good night as effusively as if I'd known him all my life, I went out to earn my pay. The fresh air made me suddenly realise that I wasn't as sober as I might have been. I wasn't drunk, but I was more than halfway there.

I wandered up the street past the house once more. The coach lamps were lit, and there was a light showing through the curtains of the downstairs room. There were a few neat plastic dustbins in the road which was a pretty good indication that there was no back entrance to any of the houses. This would have upset me normally as it was far too early to be sure that people wouldn't still be out and about. But in my present state of alcoholic euphoria, I could see no problems.

Then I had the best idea of the day. Why pussyfoot around outside? Why not bang on the front door and confront Dunning with whatever I found inside? Then I could use my natural talent for such things to provide him with enough rope to hang himself. I realise now that it was the booze doing the thinking, and even if things *hadn't* turned out the way they did, it was still a bloody fool thing to do. But it was ten o'clock, and in half an hour Mary would be expecting me. I had a momentary picture of her which somehow became mixed up with a picture of the girl at the bar. The aphrodisiacal effect of this double vision was all I needed to push me over the edge.

Although normally I'm not a bad enquiry agent, everyone is entitled to drop a brick occasionally. Hindsight has since shown me that I had already dropped it, at about five past eleven that morning. Whatever I had decided to do while I was making up my mind whether to ring the doorbell or not, it would have made no difference to what was to follow.

There was a small gate, and six feet of paved garden in front of the house. I stepped over the gate, straddling it, which showed how near drunk I was, and walked up to the front door.

I rang the bell, prepared for all eventualities. If Alworthy answered I would ask for Dunning, and if Dunning answered I would ask for Alworthy. One way or another I would get into the house, then, with one or two devastating observations I would reduce them both to the condition where they would agree to anything. If no one answered, I was prepared to lean on the doorbell all night. Or at least until half past ten.

As it turned out, things didn't go that way at all. I'd hardly touched the bell before the door was flung open by a person I assumed was Alworthy. He was about twenty-four years old, dark and willowy. He was wearing a tan coloured silk shirt with pale olive slacks. I could tell he was wearing make-up because he had been crying and his mascara had run.

"Thank God you've come," he said, and disappeared through a door that led off from the tiny hall. I stepped through the front door. I had been right about the guardsmen, there were pictures of them all over the hall. I followed him through the door into the main room. It seemed expected of me. It was a pretty room, in keeping with its owner. There were chintzy things scattered here and there, lots of low chairs and gaily coloured cushions, and a long settee at right angles to the fireplace.

In a small alcove, there was the dining table and the remains of dinner. Right again—two candles stuck in chianti bottles.

I stood in the door and looked at Alworthy, who was looking at me. The silence between us grew until I felt I had better say something.

"Mr. Alworthy..." I started.

"Well *do* something," he said petulantly.

I must have looked as vague as I felt.

"It's too bad," he said when he realised I wasn't going to be any help. "I call for the police, and they send me... oh really, it's *too* bad."

He had called the police. For what? I looked around. There was no sign of Dunning. Then I realised what it was that had been worrying me since I had first come into the room. It was the decorations; they weren't right somehow. There was too much red splashed about without regard to form or design.

The alcohol I had drunk evaporated suddenly, leaving me stone-cold sober.

I rubbed a finger along a particularly vivid splash of red which crawled down the wall just inside the door.

"It's blood," I said, sounding like an idiot.

Alworthy nearly burst into tears again.

"Of course it's blood," he wailed.

Then I realised that he had moved to the corner of the settee in order to show me something behind it. I had no desire to know what it was, but I looked nevertheless.

Dunning was crouched on his side, his knees drawn up to his chest, his hands cupping his chin. He looked as though he were trying to hide. I touched him tentatively with the toe of my shoe and regretted it immediately. He rolled from his crouched position on to his back, his hands slipping away from his chin.

I realised then that he hadn't been cupping his chin at all. The poor sod had been trying to hold his head on. There was a gash in his throat as wide as an open grave, and damn near as deep.

I was perched on the edge of an armchair when Inspector Diaman arrived, trying to look as though I had every right in the world to be there. The place was already swarming with forensics, fingerprinters, photographers and uniformed men. Two of the latter were keeping a sharp eye on me, but I was far too worried to be any trouble. I was in it up to my armpits and it was getting worse every minute.

My main cause of concern was Peter Alworthy, or to be more precise, the lack of Peter Alworthy. A moment after I had turned Dunning over and he had grinned at us with his throat, Alworthy had excused himself hurriedly for the purpose of throwing up. He had disappeared in the direction of the kitchen and that had been the last I, or anyone else, had seen of him. My observation about there being no back way out of the house had been detection of a similar order to the rest of my performance that day. There *was* a back way out and Alworthy had used it with alacrity. Two minutes after he had left me, and before I had even begun to get suspicious, the police had gonged up to the front door. They had found me poking around the living-room looking for God knows what. I had started to explain about Alworthy but they had told me to save it until Inspector Diaman arrived. They said it with such relish that I expected Torquemada to walk in the door. Perhaps I would have been better off if he had.

His arrival was announced by everyone in the room falling silent. I looked towards the door, and there he was. One of the uniformed men moved over to speak to him, and while he was doing that, I saw Diaman's eyes lift towards me. They were flat, slate grey, with no expression whatsoever. I'd never come across him before, but I had heard plenty. He was one of those policemen who subscribed to the theory that to do his job properly it was necessary to put the fear of God into the criminal classes. If he thumped a man occasionally, it was only so that man would spread the word that Diaman was a very hard case indeed. Law breakers of the lower orders had been known to give themselves up *en masse* when they heard that Diaman had been assigned to their case.

Now the uniformed man stepped back and Diaman came into the room. He ignored me completely. He had a word with the doctor, he looked at the body, he gave permission for it to be removed, he spoke to one of the fingerprint men, he instructed the photographers to pay particular attention to the disposition of the bloodstains, he had another word with the doctor, and then he disappeared for a few minutes to look over the rest of the house. Apart from that first flat stare from the door, he hadn't looked at me once. It was twenty minutes before he condescended to acknowledge my presence.

He sat down opposite me, pulling a chair forward. He looked at me sadly for a moment, then he sighed gently and started.

"Tell me all about it, son," he said. I could probably have given him a year or two, but if he wanted to call me "son", that was his affair.

"Where shall I start?" I said like an idiot.

"Start where you like, son," he said. "One way or another, we'll get it all."

And get it all he did. My training and background has given me pretty methodical thought processes, and I presented him with all the facts, starting with Danielle's visit that morning. It's all very well to be ethical and respect the anonymity of your client, but when it comes to my own hide, I can pitch to the wolves with the best of them.

I was brief, lucid and to the point. He didn't take his eyes off me for a second. He didn't nod, he didn't grunt. He just sat there like a monolithic sponge, soaking it all up. I finished and sat back, waiting for a pat on the head. He continued to stare at me, and I could almost hear the gears clicking in that steel trap he used as a mind. Then he grunted something unintelligible and heaved himself to his feet.

He walked to the door and said something to the uniformed man. Then without a backward glance, he walked out of the front door. I judged that now was the time for me to do the same. I got to my feet and headed for the door. The uniformed man grinned at me, hoping I'd cause trouble.

"Going somewhere, sir?" he said pleasantly.

"Home?" I said.

"Not just yet," he said.

Ten minutes later, I was in the interview room at the police station. Someone took my coat, someone else brought me a cup of tea, and someone else gave me a cigarette. Everyone was so damned pleasant that I began to realise just how much trouble I was in.

I waited for half an hour under the bored scrutiny of a young copper who did me the favour of not trying to start a conversation.

"May I use the telephone?" I said finally.

"I'll ask," he said and disappeared. He came back with the station sergeant.

"Who do you want to phone?" said the sergeant.

"A friend," I said, thinking of Mary.

"I'll ask the inspector," he said.

Two minutes later, he returned with a phone which he plugged in.

"Give me the number and I'll get it for you," he said.

"I've changed my mind," I said. I didn't want Mary dragged into this mess, and having met Diaman, I knew that she would be if I'd given them the slightest lead.

"The Inspector won't like that," said the sergeant. I felt like telling him what the inspector could do with himself, but I wasn't angry enough yet. But I was beginning to get that way, not with the police, but with myself. I had behaved like a first-class nut, first in ringing the doorbell, second in going into the house, and third in allowing Alworthy to get away. I should have stuck with him even if he *had* been going to throw up.

Half an hour later, Diaman sent for me. I was taken upstairs to his office. The first thing I noticed was the presence of a stenographer. Diaman saw me looking at him nervously.

"Just to make a few notes, son," he said.

"I know what he's for," I said.

"Makes it easier it all round," he said. "Sit you down."

I sat me down and waited for him to start talking.

"What sort of business do you do, son?" he asked.

"I told you, I'm a private investigator," I said.

"I know," he said. "But what do you do mostly?"

"Divorces," I said.

"Like tonight?"

"Like tonight."

"Suppose you start at the beginning again. Tell me the story like you did earlier."

If he was expecting me to make a mistake, he was going to be disappointed. I had been telling the truth before, all I had to do was tell it again. I did so, step by step, exactly as I had done before.

"You've got a good memory," he said when I finished.

"It's part of my job," I said.

"It's an interesting story," he said. "Now let's go into it in a little more detail."

I noticed that he had stopped calling me "son".

"I accept the fact that you're a private investigator," he said. "And I accept the fact that your wife..."

"My ex-wife," I interrupted.

"...your ex-wife visited you this morning. Do you know why I accept this?"

"You asked her," I said brightly.

"No, I didn't. I can't get in touch with her. But I asked your receptionist Miss Roberts. She confirms that you had an appointment with Mrs. Dunning this morning."

So Miss Roberts had been contacted. What a marvelous time she would have with Stubbs tomorrow.

"Next you went to the address she gave you and there you identify Dunning so that you would recognise him later."

"Right," I said.

"Next you follow Dunning to Alworthy's house," he said.

"Right," I said.

"Wrong," he said. I waited for him to enlarge on it.

"The house you followed him to belongs to Dunning himself, not Alworthy."

It was a surprise, but not catastrophic. It just meant that Dunning paid the rent for his boyfriend.

"I didn't check the lease," I said.

"I did," said Diaman.

"Is it important?" I said, not seeing how it could be.

"We'll see," said Diaman. "Next, you kill a couple of hours in the pub up the road. Why?"

"I was hungry and thirsty, and it was too soon for anything to happen at the house."

"Anything like what?"

"I was there to collect evidence for a divorce. The best sort of evidence would have been to find them in bed together."

"Dunning and Alworthy?" he said.

"Exactly," I said, wondering where this was leading to.

"So after two hours you leave the pub, walk up to the front door and ring the bell."

I nodded unhappily.

"So if they *had* been in bed together, one of them would have had to get up to answer the door."

"I didn't say I would find them in bed, I just said that would have been the best sort of evidence."

"But by ringing the doorbell you would automatically destroy such evidence," he said. To this observation I, of course, had no answer.

He allowed the silence to grow to embarrassing proportions before he continued. I could see the stenographer chewing the side of a fingernail while he waited for his lord and master to start again.

"The door was opened by Alworthy," he said finally.

I nodded.

"He told you to come in. It is your idea that he mistook you for the police whom he had recently telephoned, and he left you alone with the body while he went out to the kitchen to vomit."

"That's what he said," I said.

Diaman now put his hand flat on the desk and cleared his throat. Something about the way that he did it made me worried about what was coming next.

"There are certain factors about your story about which I am not happy," he said. It was the understatement of the year.

"First, Alworthy and Dunning couldn't have dined together. There was only the remains of one meal at the dining table."

"Perhaps one of them wasn't hungry," I said helpfully.

"Secondly, the call to the police did not come from the house but from a telephone booth some way down the road. A passer-by reported seeing a man trying to force an entry. So we can assume that Alworthy didn't make the call himself. Thirdly, there is no evidence that anyone apart from Dunning, was ever in the house this evening. Fourthly, what happened to Alworthy? Now you're a reasonably intelligent man. What sort of conclusion should I draw from all that?"

I knew, but he could have broken my arm before I'd have said it. So I said nothing, and he provided his own answer.

"There is not and there never has been, any such person as Alworthy," he said. And as far as he was concerned, that just about wrapped it up.

Police station cells are pretty fair as cells go. Mine had a bed, a table and a chair. For washing or going to the toilet, I had to bang on the door and a middle-aged policeman would let me out and accompany me to where I wanted to go. He would stand with me while I did it, then he would take me back and lock me up again.

I had some cigarettes and coffee sent down from the canteen and I reviewed the general situation. From whichever direction I looked at it, it was murky. I tried ticking off the essential points as I came to them.

One: I hadn't been charged with anything. Not a particularly good sign in itself, but at least better than if I *had* been. Two: the problem of the non-existent Alworthy. Non-existent as far as the police were concerned. All the facts pointed to his having done the killing and my interrupting him before he could get away. This being the case he wasn't likely to turn up out of the blue to confirm my story. Three: where was Danielle? Diaman had told me he had tried to contact her, but didn't really know where to start because the only address he had for her was the house where the killing took place. It seemed that the address she had given me for Alworthy was her own, hers and Dunning's. This didn't help my story any, because if it was her own house, why had she given the address to me as the one to follow Dunning to? Four: as long as I was locked up here, I wasn't going to be able to sort out items two and three. And until I could sort them out, I wasn't going to be able to get out of here. Five: I'd had a hell of a day, it was now two o'clock in the morning and I was tired.

So I finished my coffee and went to bed.

Diaman came down to see me at seven thirty in the morning. He too had been on the premises all night, but unlike me, he hadn't slept. He looked like hell.

He stood aside as the door was unlocked.

"Out," he said.

I picked up my jacket and tie and followed him. We went to the interview room. While I was tying my tie in front of the wall mirror, he sat and scowled at me.

"You're a lucky bastard," he said finally.

"You've found Alworthy," I said.

"Don't come that balls with me," he said. He was very angry.

"You fellows think you can get up to whatever you bloody well like. But I'm telling you, Smith, if our paths cross again, look out, because I'm going to jump on you, and jump so hard I'll break your bloody back."

I believed him too, even if I didn't understand him. What I did understand was that I was getting out. Something had come up in the night, something that Diaman didn't like. He wasn't the sort of copper who would get angry just because a prime suspect is found to be clean.

That took a vindictive copper, and he wasn't that. Therefore, he must still believe I'm as guilty as hell. So why was he releasing me?

But I wasn't going to look a gift horse in the mouth. I kept quiet while he continued to snarl at me inwardly. Then I slipped on my jacket, opened the door of the interview room and walked out. The desk sergeant looked up politely when I spoke to him.

"May I have my raincoat please," I said.

"No, you bloody can't," said Diaman from the door of the interview room. "It's got bloodstains all over it. Someone might think you've committed a crime."

This was the first I had heard of the bloodstains. But on considering the amount of blood splattered all over the murder room, it wasn't surprising. No wonder he was so needled at having me walk out of the place.

I turned right outside the station meaning to pick up a taxi to get me home. There was a black Humber parked at the kerb, and as I approached it, the door opened and a man stepped out.

The whole bloody thing fell into place there and then. I damn near turned back to take my chances with Diaman. But the man was leaning against the car smiling at me, and I knew he wouldn't let me.

"Hello, Johnny," he said affably.

"Hello, Max," I said.

CHAPTER TWO

HADN'T seen Max for five years. That wasn't strange because unless you were in the Service you didn't see Max. The last time I had seen him, I had been facing him across his desk. I had stated my case very simply, I wanted out. And he, just as simply, said I couldn't go.

I told him I was sick of the Service, sick of him, and most of all sick of myself.

"We all get low at times, John," he said. "You'll get over it."

"I know I will," I said. "That's why I want out."

"Sit down and tell me about it," he said, adopting his confessor role. I didn't have to tell him, he already knew. But he thought the effect of laying it out on the line might act as a catharsis. I knew the only effective catharsis for me was a lobotomy, but I told him all about it anyway.

I had been back from Algeria for a week, and still I couldn't sleep for more than an hour at a stretch. The whole job had been such a monumental cock up from start to finish, that it was a wonder there was anyone left alive to talk about it. Privately, I knew, Max regretted this fact. He would have preferred a nice clean end to the affair with no loose ends. I was a loose end.

Some anonymous clerk had given the operation the code name Redskin. And that just about covered it. Skin red with blood, floors and ceilings swimming in it, heels skidding in pools of it. Blood over everything, blood on my hands that even after a week's scouring I couldn't seem to scrub off.

MAKE CONTACT WITH ALI BEN AHMED, ASSIST IN ELIMINATING THE LAGRAVE FACTOR.

That's how the order filtered down to me, and that's what I set out to do. The Lagrave factor was the name given to a group of mis-guided Frenchmen who, under the mask of the Algerie Francaise movement, were laying the foundations for a Red intervention in Algeria. At least, that's what we had been told.

The Arab Bureau in Algeria couldn't go to the French Bureau, because they were virtually at war with each other, so the whole operation landed on our plate. As long as France and Algeria were fighting each other with no third-party interference, it was no concern of ours. But as soon as information came to hand that there *was* third-party interest, and who that third party was, then something had to be done.

So I packed my little bag and left with George Barnes, another Service man with whom I'd worked before. The opera-tion had been simple, Ali ben Ahmed took time off from slaugh-tering Frenchmen to show us where and how the renegades were operating. In a week we had the whole thing sewn up. It was too easy, a factor that worried me until I found out the reason, and then it worried me even more. They were amateurs, little more than kids. Embroiled in a war they didn't really under-stand, they had been a soft touch for the third party. Pictures had been painted of a new, free Algeria owing allegiance neither to Mother France nor the corrupt Arab government who would take over when the French left. And these poor, deluded infants lapped it up.

The normal procedure for eliminating a subversive cell is to first search out the tendrils that radiate from the core. Then when the core is eliminated, the tendrils can be wrapped up quietly, without any fuss. It took George and me four days to discover that there were no tendrils. There was nothing more than a group of kids printing and distributing communist propaganda, which nobody bothered to read anyway.

I sent a cable to London stressing that somewhere along the line we'd been fooled. The Service had been dragged into something for some other purpose than the one stated. It took Max two days to run the whole dirty business to earth. The third party had leaked the information to Ali ben Ahmed, knowing he would get on to London. Then the presence of Service personnel on French territory would be leaked to the French Bureau and a fine old *schemozzle* would result, considerably straining the *entente cordiale* and the Franco-British Nato relations.

But thanks to my cable, Max managed to jump on the scheme before it bore fruit. Two third-party agents in Paris disappeared, and the leak to the French didn't take place. But by now there were a lot of worried men in London, and somewhere along the line, someone panicked. Max was ordered to remove all evidence and get us out of Algeria fast. As far as Max was concerned, people were evidence, and in reply to my cable that the third-party cell should be let off with smacked bottoms, I received a cryptic message from London.

ELIMINATE. MAX.

And we eliminated. Armed with sawn-off shotguns, George, myself and two of Ahmed's men forced an entry into the old house they used as their headquarters. There were twelve of them, not one over twenty years old, and four of them girls.

One girl particularly I noticed, probably because she was the youngest and prettiest. She had long, straight blonde hair, and she was wearing blue slacks and a blue silk shirt. She was making coffee when we arrived, while her companions were moving around sorting out pamphlets, and manning an old printing press in the corner.

Like all the others, she turned towards us as we suddenly appeared among them. Her blue eyes which matched her silk shirt, were wide with enquiry. I wanted to tell her not to worry, that everything would be all right. Then a boy standing close to her, realised what we were going to do, and grabbed at a gun in his belt. I shot him. A sawn-off shotgun isn't the most selective of weapons, that's why we were using them. I killed the boy all right, and I also blew the pretty girl's face off.

In thirty seconds, it was all over. George had a bullet in his chest which was scheduled to kill him half an hour later, and one of our Arabs was nursing a shattered elbow. The other Arab was moving about the room finishing with a knife what the guns had started.

The pretty girl wasn't dead and I wanted to do something for her. Give her a new face perhaps to replace the one I had removed. She lay in a pool of blood making a small whimpering sound and moving her hands spasmodically. Then the Arab leaned over her and deftly slit her throat. He looked up at me and grinned. Another second and I would have shot him, too, but fortunately I chose that moment to be sick. The trouble was that we were unable to get out of that place until the truck we had arranged for arrived to clear out the bodies. And the truck was late, half an hour late. So for half an hour I sat with George while he died, and all around me the young people lay in their own blood, looking like pale orchids on a field of scarlet.

Five hours later, I was back in London. By then I had developed a Lady Macbeth complex. I couldn't stop washing my hands. The psychiatrist told me that it would go away after a few months and I should ask Max for a transfer in the meantime, to some desk job out of the field. I didn't ask him for a bloody thing. I told him I was getting out altogether. When he told me he couldn't allow that, I told him to go and stuff himself. We argued back and forth for a couple of days, but he couldn't shift me. He had to let me go if I insisted, and I insisted. I commuted my pension rights into a lump sum, collected a couple of months' back pay and went on a bender which culminated in kicking my wife out of the house. I never saw Max again. Not until now.

He's a small man physically, with thinning hair and a sharply defined face, all planes and angles. He has a thin, humourless mouth and very good teeth. His eyes are prominent and he's a permanent martyr to conjunctivitis. He uses eye drops as frequently as another man uses a pocket handkerchief, pulling out a small bottle and squeezing the drops into the corners of his eyes.

He did this as I sat across from him in the office I had hoped never to see again. Then he sniffed hard, put the bottle away and looked at me, his eyes swimming.

"Sorry about that," he said. "Same old trouble."

I said nothing.

"You're in a spot of bother," he said.

"You should know," I said. "You got me out of it."

"I did, didn't I? He's quite a bulldog that Diaman. Once he gets his teeth in, he hates to let go. I had to pull some very well-connected strings."

"Why?" I said.

He continued as though he hadn't heard me.

"For a couple of hours last night I didn't think I'd be able to pull it off. But now, here you are."

"Why?" I persisted.

He looked at me levelly. His eyes had stopped watering.

"You know why, John," he said. "I want the notebook."

"What notebook?" I said.

He sighed and scratched the corner of his chin. He needed a shave, I noticed, but then so did I.

"We're professionals," he said finally. "You can fool some of the people all the time, but you can fool the professionals hardly any of the time."

"I'm not trying to fool anyone," I said.

"Then turn over the notebook like a good fellow, and we'll forget all about it."

"What will you do if I don't?" I said.

He looked genuinely concerned.

"Don't say that, John," he said. "I told you I had to pull some important strings on your behalf. I'd hate to see all that effort go to waste."

I was way ahead of him.

"If I let you have the notebook, I'm clean. If I don't, I go back to Diaman," I said.

"That's about it," he said.

"Just say I *do* let you have the notebook," I said. "Who gets the chop for Dunning?"

"The file is marked 'unsolved'." he said.

"Then I'd better let you have it," I said.

He smiled.

"There's a good chap. Just tell me where it is and I'll have it picked up."

"Can't do that," I said. "Must pick it up myself."

He thought about this for a moment, then he shrugged.

"So be it," he said. "When can I expect you?"

"When you see me," I said. I got to my feet. He let me get as far as the door before he spoke again.

"Not like you, John," he said. "A messy job, not like you at all."

"I like to cut throats," I said, and left.

I called in at home where I showered, shaved and changed my clothes. Then I took a taxi to Marylebone Station. I caught an Amersham train, and at the first stop I pretended to be asleep until the train started to move out of the station. Then I made a good show of waking up suddenly like a man who realises he's nearly overslept his destination. The train was doing ten miles an hour and gaining speed fast as I opened the carriage door and jumped out. I just made the end of the platform where it started to slope down to track level. Needless to say, no one got out after me. I thought I had seen a man someway down the carriage look startled when I suddenly erupted, but he could hardly pull the communication cord, and I may have been wrong anyway.

I left the station and walked out into the small town. There I caught a bus to Uxbridge, where I took the Underground back into London. I changed trains and got out at Victoria main line station. There I bought a ticket to Box Hill.

At Box Hill station there were no taxis, so I walked the two miles to Gunther's house. His daughter let me in and said the old man would be glad to see me. She wasn't so glad; she disapproved of me strongly.

Gunther was sitting up in bed wearing flannel pyjamas and an embroidered shawl over his massive shoulders. Even now, after six years in bed, he still emanated strength and vitality. His blue eyes twinkled from either side of his great beaked nose, and his hand, when he gripped mine, did so gently so as not to crack any bones. There was a wooden bar rigged up over the bed, and he used to exercise on this daily, pulling himself up and lowering himself for hours on end. He had no further use for his giant strength, but he kept at it just the same. Below the waist of course there was nothing. A bullet had shattered the base of his spine and paralysed everything below. His legs were like matchsticks, and even if he had been able to stand, they would no longer have been able to bear the weight of his hugely over-developed torso.

As always, he was genuinely glad to see me. For ten minutes, he complained bitterly that it had been more than three months since my last visit. Even after twenty years in England, he hadn't lost the heavy accent of his own country. I sat listening to his complaints like a penitent schoolboy. He grew bored with it after a while.

"So how is the peeping tom business?" he asked finally.

"It's a living," I said.

"What sort of living," he said, his voice full of scorn. "A living by looking in bedroom windows."

"I saw Max this morning," I said.

"Ah," he said slowly. "So now we get down to it."

"I think I'm in trouble," I said.

"I think so too," he said. "Or you wouldn't be here. Tell me."

I told him, exactly as I had told Diaman, but continuing the story so that it included my interview with Max.

He was silent when I finished, and I sat there waiting patiently.

"The notebook," he said. "You know nothing of it?"

"Nothing," I said.

"This man Dunning worked in the Foreign Office. Max is interested. Therefore, the contents of the notebook must be classified."

I nodded. Gunther sorted out the facts in his mind, his eyes going blank with concentration. Then he relaxed.

"So we have a situation," he said. "The situation is this. There is a notebook which Dunning owned and in which he had written certain information. Dunning is killed for possession of the notebook, and you have done the killing, therefore you now have the notebook. Why do you want the notebook? You want to sell it for a big price. The price must be big because the book is valuable enough for very important strings to be pulled to release you, when you should be charged with murder."

"Right," I said. "Except that I didn't do the killing and I haven't got the notebook."

"But you didn't tell this to Max," he said.

"No."

"Why not?"

"The notebook got me out of serious trouble. If Max thought I didn't have it, he'd throw me back in."

"Whereas now he thinks you are going to get it for him and everything will be O.K."

I nodded.

"Then you must get it," he said. "Without it you will be hanged."

"They don't hang people anymore," I said.

"You'd rather go to prison for twenty-five years?" said Gunther.

"I'd rather neither," I said.

"So now we come to Mr. Alworthy," said Gunther. "We assume that he too knew of the notebook and he killed Dunning to get it. Question: has he got it yet? Answer: no."

"Why?" I asked.

"You interrupted him," he said. "If he had already found the notebook, he would not have been there when you arrived."

"Reasonable," I said.

"So you must find it before Alworthy does," said Gunther.

"And give it to Max," I said.

"Maybe, maybe not. Read it first, find out what all the fuss is about. A man dead with his throat cut, a man released from jail when he should be charged with murder. We all know Max. Perhaps the notebook will provide you with a little insurance for your old age, because once you give it back to him, then it is unlikely that you will have an old age."

He nodded his head slowly, liking the idea.

"Find out what is in the book," he said. "*Then* decide what you are going to do."

I thought about this for a moment, then Gunther brought up a factor I had been trying to ignore.

"Danielle," he said. "You've thought about her?"

"She may have been genuine," I said.

"I think it is stretching coincidence further than I like to. Go and see her."

"I don't know where she is," I said.

"Find out. Talk to her. Don't tell her anything, but listen to what she has to say. Make up your mind afterwards."

After that, we talked of other things for an hour. His daughter brought us some lunch on trays, and later she chased me out of the place. As I shook his hand before leaving, he pulled me forward and planted a great wet kiss on the side of my face. He always did it, and it always embarrassed me momentarily. That's why he did it.

"You English," he said. "You are ashamed of emotion between men. You think it is pansy to kiss another man. You are my son, I am your father, so I kiss you."

He wasn't my father, but he was all the father I had, and since his own boy had been killed just before the end of the war, I had taken his place in the old man's affections. I didn't mind, in fact I was bloody glad of it. He'd saved my life once on a job in Finland, and I'd done the same for him a couple of years later. At least our affection for each other was by choice and not forced on us by accident of birth.

On my way back to London, I considered his advice. It was good, as always. That's why I discussed things with him. I would probably have done what he suggested anyway, but I felt better knowing it was what *he* would have done in my place.

He had been the best operative the Service ever had. After the bullet had killed his usefulness, Max had wanted him deported under the Aliens Order. Gunther was Finnish and in Helsinki he would have gone to jail at worst or become a starving cripple at best. Fortunately, I had got wind of Max's plan, and I had threatened to scream so loud, that Max had been forced to back down. Then, in case he should change his mind, I had spirited Gunther away to the place in Box Hill. I'd done it so damn well, it had taken Max eight months to locate him. By that time, Max had cooled down sufficiently that I knew I wouldn't have to worry any more. Added to that, I had started keeping my "Dossier on Max," a fact which I managed to leak to him, and which put the fear of Christ into him.

Gunther still drew his government pension and it was sufficient for him and his daughter to live on. And although his body was now useless, his mind was as sharp as ever. He pretended he had never forgiven me for quitting the Service, but secretly he was glad. He had seen the mess I was in after the Algerian incident.

It was raining when I reached Victoria, and now possessing no raincoat, I treated myself to a taxi home. I'd hardly opened the door when the phone started to ring. I decided not to answer it, then I changed my mind. It was Mary, who only rang me when there was an earthquake or the sun exploded.

"Can I see you?" she said.

"Is it important?" I asked. It was a stupid question.

"Come round at seven," she said.

It must have been important. There was a standing order that I never tried to contact her before eight in case her boss, who always drove her home from work, hadn't left the flat.

I promised to be there. It wasn't too much of an inconvenience. What I had to do that evening couldn't be done until much later.

When she hung up, I rang the office.

"No," said Miss Roberts. "No messages. Mr. Stubbs has signed up a new singer. He discovered him in a coffee bar, just like Tommy Steele."

I hoped he would be as successful, then Stubbs could start coughing up his half of the rent. But I didn't say this to Miss Roberts; she would have thought it disloyal.

I made a quick call on my way to Mary's place to pick up a few things I hadn't thought I'd ever need again. I left them in the car, and went in to see Mary. She lived in one of those genteel, faded houses in Belgravia. Like its neighbours, it had been turned into apartments, some with their own bathrooms and kitchenettes, some without. Mary's was with, a large high room, warm and comfortable.

The street door was open and I walked up the wide curved staircase, a relic of a bygone elegance, to the first floor where Mary had her apartment. I tapped on the door and heard her call for me to come in. The door was on the latch and I slipped the latch back into place before closing it behind me.

"I'm in the bath," she called.

I picked up the evening paper and was about to sit down and wait, when she called me again.

"Come in," she said.

I went into the bathroom and sat on the lavatory. She looked and smelled very sexy in the bath, and I started to think about things I had no business thinking about considering the trouble I was in.

"How's the water?" I said brightly, hoping she'd invite me in to try. But she didn't. She looked at me steadily for a moment, her eyes wide and clear.

"What are you up to?" she said.

"You, if you'll give me half a chance," I said.

She grinned, but only with her mouth.

"I had visitors last night," she said.

"Oh," I said. There didn't seem much else I could say.

"They wanted to know if you'd left anything here," she said.

"Like what?"

"Like an overnight bag," she said.

"You're my overnight bag," I said, trying to make light of something which was plucking at the hairs at the back of my neck. "Who were they?"

"They said they were from the police," she said.

"But you didn't believe them," I said.

"No. Yes, I did. No, I didn't... I don't know," she said.

That meant that they probably weren't policemen. Real policemen wouldn't have left that much area for doubt.

"What did you tell them?" I said.

"I told them you haven't got an overnight bag, and even if you had, you wouldn't leave it here."

"And...?"

"They were very polite. Please could they have a look. They were neat and tidy, they put everything back in its place. They scared the shit out of me."

Mary rarely used bad language, an indication of just how much shit they'd scared out of her.

"What were they like?" I said.

"I told you, they were very polite. They went all through my underwear cupboard and didn't bat an eyelid. They even looked under the mattress. Then they made the bed again for me afterwards."

"Why did they frighten you?"

"They were so impersonal. They behaved as if I wasn't even here. One of them had a harelip."

"Can I have a drink?" I said.

"Get me one," she said.

I poured the drinks. The whole thing smelled like a cheap embalming. If they were police, how had they got on to Mary, and what were they looking for? If they weren't police, then I knew what they were looking for, but still I didn't know how they got on to Mary. I'd only been seeing her for three years, so there would have been no record of her in my Service file.

I was about to carry Mary's drink into the bathroom, when she came out wrapped in a towel. She took the drink from me and sat in one of the armchairs. The towel settled around her, protecting her modesty like a shroud. I sat down opposite her.

"I don't want to see you anymore," she said.

It was a decision I had no right to argue with.

"O.K.," I said. I finished my drink.

"Do you mind?" she said.

"Ofcourse I mind," I said.

"You can find someone else to go to bed with," she said.

It was more a question than a statement.

"Yes," I said. I stood up.

"I was really frightened," she said.

"I know," I said. I started to say something else, then I thought what the hell. I headed for the door.

"You *are* a bastard," she said.

I looked back at her. She looked smaller wrapped in that towel.

"I don't want you to be frightened," I said. "You're right, I can get laid somewhere else."

"You're rotten in bed," she said. "You won't find anyone else who'll put up with it."

"It'll be fun looking," I said.

"No, it won't," she said. "You've got a thing about it. The harder you try the worse you are. At least with me you've stopped trying."

"I don't want you to be frightened," I said.

"If I'd known what they were after, it wouldn't have been so bad."

"They won't trouble you again," I said, wishing I could believe it.

"Would you come and see me if I didn't go to bed with you?" she said.

"Yes."

She sighed.

"I know you would. That's why I can't kick you out. You're fat and you're too old for me. You're selfish, your beard scrapes me raw 'cos you only shave once a day, and you're going bald. What the hell I put up with you for, I'll never know."

I tried out a smile from the door.

"You want to mother me," I said.

She stood up and the towel fell around her feet.

"Come and be mothered then," she said.

She smelled of lavender and fresh air after her bath. I nibbled her shoulder, then whispered in her ear.

"A going away present?" I said.

"I talk too much," she said.

We went to bed and I was so good that afterwards she pulled back and looked at me.

"You've been taking lessons," she said.

I was as surprised as she was, and in case we'd both made a mistake, we confirmed our findings an hour later.

❧   ❧   ❧

I left her just after midnight. I thought that I was as near being in love with her as I had ever been. It was hell leaving the warm-smelling bed, but life's like that at times.

I drove to Victoria and left the car in Ebury Street. From there I walked. There were a few people about who seem to live out their lives close to main-line stations. If there was anyone following me, he must have been very good, far too good for me to be able to lose him, so I didn't bother taking any detours.

I walked past Dunning's house. It was closed up tight. At the end of the street I turned right and then right again down the parallel street. If I'd done that last night I wouldn't be here now, I thought. There was a small alley leading between two of the houses, and this in turn was intersected by another alley that ran along the backs of the houses in both streets. The older one gets the more one learns. I now knew that a dustbin in the front didn't mean there was no backway in, it just meant there were lazy dustmen.

There was a door let into the wall, and just so I didn't make a mistake, the house number was painted on the door in figures six inches high. The door was secured with a Yale type lock. I took something from the packet I had collected before I went to see Mary, and let myself in.

Inside was a minute garden bounded on three sides by high walls and on the fourth by the house itself. On the walls were painted views of a stately English garden. On my right, a path led half a mile down towards a tree-sheltered lake. On the left, two hundred yards away stood an oriental pavilion. The painting had been done by an expert in perspective, and in the vague light that leaked from the street, the lake looked real enough to swim in.

The back door was more difficult than the one to the garden. It was bolted on the inside. So I left it alone and went in through the kitchen window. Inside I put my foot in the sink, which still held last night's dirty dishes. The clatter was awful, and a dog started barking next door. By the time I had sorted myself out, the dog's master had succeeded in shouting it into silence again, the shouting effectively masking the rest of the noise I made getting in.

I crunched my way across broken crockery to the living-room. My pencil flashlight showed me that the place had been tidied up since last night. Some attempt had been made to scrub the blood off the walls, but complete redecoration was the only thing that would remove the last traces of the outgoing tenant.

The place had been searched of course. The books had been replaced on their shelves far too neatly, and there was still soot in the fireplace where somebody had probed up the chimney. The stairs were narrow and the bedroom opened directly from the top of the staircase. The bathroom lay beyond the bedroom.

I pulled open a drawer in the long dresser. It was full of Danielle's underwear, neatly and methodically placed in little piles, brassieres on the left, pants on the right, stockings in the middle. That meant they'd searched up here too. Danielle had always treated her personal possessions with a casual disregard for order that had made me grind my teeth at times, and five years isn't long enough to change the habits of a lifetime.

I thought for a moment of the patient, methodical men who must have spent the day taking the house apart. They would have slit all the upholstery neatly along its seams, and then sewn it up again afterwards; they would have tapped the walls and removed the skirting boards; they would have dismantled the electrical fitments, and reassembled them; they would have unscrewed the wall mirrors; they would have taken off the panels from the bath, drained the lavatory cistern, emptied the storage tank, and then still not finding what they were looking for, they would have put everything right again. Large, patient men, experts who knew what they were looking for.

Me, I didn't even know, but I had the edge on them nevertheless. I knew where to look.

On the dressing table among the scent bottles and cream jars there was a small Victorian jewel box, a present from me to Danielle when I had still thought a time would come when I would be able to buy her jewels. I ran my hand down the studs at the rear of the box and a small flat drawer at the bottom snapped open. It was empty. Danielle was saving it for the important piece of jewelry which I had never bought her, and which Dunning certainly wasn't going to be able to. Lots of these old Victorian pieces have secret drawers, a fact that the methodical searchers would be well aware of. But, again, I had the edge, because the thing that had really endeared me to this particular piece of cabinetmakers' art, was that the secret drawer had a secret drawer. It was necessary to remove the first drawer completely and use a pencil or pen to probe in the cavity for a small stud which released a catch so that the back of the cabinet fell outwards, revealing a narrow cavity just wide enough to hold a few banknotes or papers or, in this case, a flat, black, plastic-covered notebook.

CHAPTER THREE

I WENT to an all-night cafe in the Bayswater Road. Armed with a cup of tea and a Wimpey, I tucked myself into a corner table. I mopped the dregs of tea and coffee from the table top with a paper napkin, and opened the notebook for the first time.

Whatever it was saying, it started right out on page one without any form of heading. I read the first line:

24XB379yrc47aab986YYbBV

The rest of the page was like that. So was the second and the twenty-second. I flipped through to the end. The last fifteen pages were blank. I turned back to page one and looked at it until I was bug-eyed. In the old days I had known something about code, not much, but sufficient to know that without a key of some sort it's next to impossible to break down even the simplest cypher. This one wasn't simple.

I paid for my tea and Wimpey and took a taxi to Piccadilly Circus. I went into the all-night chemist and at the stationery counter I bought two notebooks as near similar to the one I had found as possible. From there, I walked to the all-night post office, where I bought two registered envelopes. I spent half an hour scribbling a mass of letters and figures into the two books I had just bought, then I put the real notebook and one of the phonies into the registered envelopes. I addressed them and posted them. The other phony notebook I tucked into my inside jacket pocket. The receipts for the postal registration I tore up and dropped in the wastepaper basket on my way out. I took a taxi back to Ebury Street, where I picked up the car and drove home.

I let myself into the flat, cold and tired. In the last twenty-four hours I'd had about three hours' sleep, and that in a police cell. I'd lost my raincoat, and while it wasn't much as coats go, it was all I had. All I wanted now was a hot bath, a large drink, and fourteen hours' sleep. What I got was a kick in the balls as I closed the door behind me. It wasn't too hard a kick, just hard enough to make me want to die quickly, and not hard enough to enable me to do so. I was so busy nursing myself for the next five minutes, that I didn't even look at the man who had kicked me. When I did, it wasn't too much of a surprise. It was Alworthy. He was sitting in my best armchair, holding on his lap a very large gun. At least it seemed large from where I was looking, the hole of the barrel gaping at me like the entrance to Blackwall tunnel. There was no silencer on the gun, a fact which didn't make me feel any better. The true professional doesn't use a silencer. It's bulky, it decreases accuracy, and it is generally more trouble than it is worth. Few people know what a gun sounds like. You can fire one in Oxford Street at high noon, and take money that no one will recognise the sound for what it is. Alworthy knew this, and so he didn't bother with a silencer. Funny, he didn't look queer any more, he just looked mean.

He watched me put myself together with an interested detachment, as though he were a spectator and not the cause. He allowed me to drag myself to my feet and lurch over to the sideboard where I kept the booze. Fortunately, the bottle was on top of the sideboard. If I had been forced to reach inside, he would probably have shot me. I unscrewed the cap from the vodka bottle and took a belt that went straight down to my crotch. It didn't help much, but enough for me to unbend myself a little. I took another belt, slower this time. Then I put the bottle down carefully, screwed the top back on, and prepared to meet my doom.

"Sit down," he said. I sat.

"Fold your arms." I folded.

"Where is it?" he said.

I didn't even have time to look innocent. He leaned forward and tapped me on the kneecap with the barrel of the gun. It wasn't quite as painful as the kick, but it was on the way. My eyes began to water. "Where is it?" he said.

I unfolded my arms very slowly, and with two fingers I dipped into my breast pocket and extracted the notebook. He watched me like a predatory hawk, the gun as solid as the rock of Gibraltar.

"On the floor," he said. I held the notebook out to drop it on the floor.

"You," he said. "Face down."

I got off the chair and lay face down on the floor. He stood up, and bending over me he placed the barrel of the gun behind my ear. With the other hand he took the notebook. I heard him flip through the pages and then the barrel of the gun was withdrawn. I tried to remember whether a bullet in the back of the head killed outright, or whether you lingered for a few seconds. My nose started to tickle with dust from the carpet and I wanted to sneeze. Instead, I spoke, my voice muffled by the carpet.

"It's the wrong book," I said.

There was a moment's silence, then I felt the gun barrel placed behind my ear again, a little harder this time.

"You're lying," he said.

"So I'm lying," I said, trying to sound as though this sort of thing happened to me every day of the week.

There was a long pause while he digested this bit of information.

Then he gave me a jab with the gun barrel that nearly took my ear off.

"Up," he said.

He moved back six feet and watched me climb to my feet. Then he poked the gun towards a chair. I sat and folded my arms again before he could tell me.

"You're not as stupid as you look," he said.

I was, but I wasn't going to let him know.

"Where is it?" he said.

"I mailed it," I said. "Registered."

"To whom?"

"To myself."

"Where?"

"Here," I said.

"When did you mail it?"

"An hour ago." It felt like a week.

He managed to glance at his watch without seeming to take his eyes off me.

"What time is your first delivery?" he said.

"Seven thirty. But it won't arrive by first delivery. Registered mail always comes second."

"What time?"

"About eleven thirty," I said.

He thought about this for a moment, then he made up his mind.

"We'll wait," he said.

The thought of spending the night gazing down the barrel of that gun didn't appeal to me much, but as an alternative to having my head blown off, it didn't seem so bad.

At six thirty, I even managed to doze off for a few minutes. Not him though. I don't think he blinked his eyes once. Looking at him sitting there I wondered how I had ever thought he was a queer. He was as hard as nails and twice as sharp. It had been the clothes he was wearing, I suppose, and the general way he had camped around. It had been a good act, and that combined with the fact that I had been conditioned to expect a queer, had been sufficient.

But Dunning must have known him as a queer, and he would have required more positive proof. I tried to visualise the man sitting opposite me in bed with Dunning. I couldn't. All I could see was Dunning with his throat cut, and Alworthy as he was now, a hard case, about as queer as James Bond.

At half past seven, he allowed me to make some coffee. While I pottered back and forth, he stood in the kitchen door watching me, looking every inch the professional. But professional what? Killer certainly, agent probably, blackmailer possibly. He treated the gun with casual respect, and his behaviour towards me had been of the highest order right from the opening kick. Disable your opponent before you attempt to deal with him. Having me lay face down on the floor was good too. He'd learned his trade, whatever that was, in a good school. It would be interesting to see what he would do when the postman arrived.

After the coffee, he suddenly became talkative.

"You used to be quite a big wheel," he said.

I had never been more than one of the hired help, but to some I suppose it might have seemed important. But it was his knowing about it that intrigued me.

"Not for a long time now," I said.

"I heard you hadn't the stomach for it," he said.

"Something like that," I said. There was something seriously wrong with security somewhere. I didn't like it.

"You fellows who work for Max are all the same," he said, compounding my concern. "Big wheels until the going gets a little rough, then you quit."

"We all make mistakes," I said.

"Not me," he said. I could believe him too.

"It all depends who you work for," I said.

He looked at me for a moment then he grinned.

"For all the good it will do you, I could tell you," he said. "But I won't. Die ignorant, die happy."

I digested this with my coffee, and went to pour myself another cup.

He followed me into the kitchen again.

"What happens when the postman comes?" he said.

"He'll ring the outside bell. I'll ask who it is on the security phone. When he tells me, I'll go downstairs and sign for the letter."

"Does the postman know you?" he said.

"Yes," I lied.

"So you'll have to sign for it yourself?"

"He might let you have it," I said. "But I doubt it."

He followed me back into the living-room, thoughtful.

After five minutes, he told me what I was going to do.

"When you speak to the postman on the security phone, tell him you're sending a friend down to sign for the letter. Tell him you've got a bad leg or something."

"He may offer to bring it up," I said.

"Even better, you can sign for it yourself."

"What happens next?" I said.

He looked at me for a moment, then he laughed.

"You certainly have been away for a long time," he said.

I should have known. It's the sort of question a professional doesn't have to ask.

We spent the next three hours looking at each other. He had decided to stop talking, and after a couple of attempts to draw something out of him, I gave up, and started to try and work out what he would do when he opened the envelope and found another phony notebook.

Long before the postman arrived, I had worked out that I was going to have to get him to come up to the flat. If I suggested that my friend go down for the letter, my friend was going to kill me before he did so. With the postman up here, there was a chance that Alworthy would open the envelope and look at the notebook before he pulled the trigger. What he would do after that was anybody's guess. The only thing I could be sure of was that it would be painful.

At eleven twenty, he looked at his watch. He wasn't nervous or even concerned. He hadn't fidgeted and this was only the second time he had checked his watch. As though on cue, the doorbell rang. He looked up at me coolly.

"He's early," he said.

"It happens," I said.

He gestured towards the security phone with the gun.

I stood up and went to the phone.

"Yes?" I said.

"Registered letter for Mr. Smith," came the disembodied voice.

"Can you bring it up," I said. "I can't get downstairs."

"On me way, guv," came the voice.

I pressed the button that opened the front door and turned to see how Alworthy was taking it. He was grinning at me.

"You're grasping at straws," he said.

"I'm drowning," I said.

He stood up and moved so that he would be behind the door when I opened it. We heard the postman labouring up the stairs, and then the pause while he identified the apartment. Then the doorbell rang, at the same time as Alworthy jabbed me hard in the side with the gun, just in case I had forgotten.

I opened the door and there was Max. Behind him stood two members of the Heavy Squad, with hands tucked deep in raincoat pockets. Before I could say or do anything, he spoke.

"Sign 'ere, Mr. Smith," he said, handing me a gun.

"Thank you," I said.

Then I closed the door gently in his face and let Alworthy see the gun I was holding.

"Snap," I said.

For one moment, it looked as though he was going to chance it, and my finger tightened fractionally on the trigger. This is a dangerous thing to do if you don't know the tension of the gun you're holding. The gun jerked in my hand, there was a noise like the crack of doom, and Alworthy slammed back against the wall as though he had been hit by a truck. I watched him as he slid down the wall leaving a smear of red on my blue distemper.

After that, there didn't seem anything left to do but let Max in.

"You might have given me a gun that didn't fire as soon as I looked at it," I said.

"Sorry, old man," he said. He looked at Alworthy whose eyes were open and whose mouth gaped like a fish.

"Is he dead?" he said.

I hefted the gun in my hand. It was a .45, sufficient to stop a small elephant in full flight.

"As if you didn't know," I said.

"Pity," he said, lying like a cheap carpet.

"I've probably killed the family next door too," I said. There was a hole in the wall where the bullet had passed through after demolishing Alworthy. I handed the gun back to Max carefully.

"The landlord's not going to like that," I said.

"We'll fix it up," he said brightly, moving across to the phone. He dialed a number.

"Petersfield," he said. The Service were still getting their daily code words from the AA handbook. He waited a moment, then he spoke again. "This is Max. One disposal squad to flat 4, 27 Earls Court Garden Square."

He hung up and turned to me.

"You *have* been busy," he said.

I went to pour myself a drink. I didn't offer him one.

"This is Alworthy I presume," he said.

"You know bloody well it is," I said.

"He won't be much help to you as far as the Dunning killing is concerned, will he."

He was right. Without Alworthy, Max had me by the short hairs.

He shook his head.

"You shouldn't have killed him," he said.

"I'm sorry," I said. "It won't happen again."

"We all make mistakes," he said. He pulled from his raincoat the notebook that Alworthy had been waiting for.

"I bumped into the postman downstairs," he said. "I thought I'd save him a climb."

"Very considerate," I said.

"You've got a lot to thank me for," he said. "Alworthy would have been very disappointed."

"I don't have to thank you for anything," I said. "If you knew he was here, why didn't you come sooner?"

"But I didn't," said Max with injured dignity. "I just assumed you'd have a registered package this morning, so I waylaid the postman. Your excuse that you couldn't get downstairs didn't sound like you at all. So I came up."

"You're a lying sod," I said. After all, I didn't work for him anymore. He shrugged.

"Have it your way," he said. He held up the notebook.

"I assume by this that you *do* have the notebook somewhere."

"I have it," I said.

"Can we go and fetch it now old man," he said.

"No old man, we can't," I said.

I was delighted to see him start to look angry. It wasn't much, a slight tightening of the mouth, but it did wonders for my morale.

"I presume you have some valid reason for refusing," he said.

"You can presume whatever you like," I said. "You'll get the notebook when I'm good and ready to give it to you."

"Don't push your luck," said Max. "Diaman would just love to get his hands on you."

"But he won't as long as I've got the notebook," I said.

"You're not thinking of going into business on your own, I hope," said Max.

"I might."

"Don't," he said.

"If I don't, it won't be because you say so," I said.

He looked at me steadily for a moment, then he relaxed. He sat down and pulled his eyedrop bottle from his pocket. He unscrewed the stopper and squeezed two drops into each eye. Then he blew his nose loudly.

"Have you any idea what you're mixed up in?" he said finally.

"Something pretty murky, if you've got anything to do with it," I said.

"I suppose it is murky," he said. "But you were in the Service, so it shouldn't surprise you."

"Was," I said.

"Once an agent always an agent," he said.

"Balls!" I said.

"Would it help you to make up your mind about the notebook if I told you all about it?" he said.

"It might."

"Dunning was going to give it to the Chinese," he said. "Alworthy had a better idea. He was going to sell it to them."

"What's in the notebook?"

"Don't you know?"

"It's in code."

He nodded. "Dunning was a cypher man in the war. We got on to him three days ago. Before we could do anything, he'd met Alworthy and got his throat cut."

"He'd met Alworthy before that," I said.

"So I understand. But we weren't watching him, so we couldn't know."

"What about Alworthy?" I said.

"Freelance," said Max. "We've got a file on him, but we didn't even know he was in the country until you turned him up."

"Everyone else seemed to know," I said.

Max shrugged.

"As Kenning, Kentish, Schmidt or Josset, we would have known him. Alworthy was a brand new identity."

I glanced at Alworthy who had stopped bleeding and was beginning to stiffen. Fat lot of good it had done him. I turned back to Max.

"You still haven't told me what was in the notebook," I said.

"It's better you don't know," said Max. "You don't want to get yourself involved."

I tried to work out how much more involved I could get. But Max was saying nothing, so I let it go.

There was a lot more I wanted to ask, but the disposal squad arrived at that point. There were four very efficient young men who nodded politely at Max, gave me an incurious glance, and set about their business. The late Peter Alworthy, Kenning, Kentish, Schmidt, Josset was laid out on a rubber sheet and undressed quickly. The clothes and the contents of his pockets were put into a bag with a drawstring top. He had suffered a cadaveric spasm at the moment of death, and it was necessary to break his hand to remove the gun. This was done with an iron bar, the sound of the bones splintering like breaking wood. Then the edges of the rubber sheet were brought together across the body and stapled together. The bundle was then put into a small laundry basket, and three of the young men carried it downstairs. The fourth fetched a bowl of warm water from the kitchen. He added some chemical which he carried in a small plastic wallet, and washed down my wall and cleaned the carpet. Then he nodded politely and departed after his fellows. He had been quiet, efficient and quick. He also had a harelip.

I made some coffee while this was going on, and unbent sufficiently to offer a cup to Max.

Finally, we were alone again.

"I'll send a plasterer along to fix that hole in the wall," he said. "We might have to redecorate."

"Be my guest," I said.

Then there was a long pause while each of us waited to see which way the other would jump.

"What are you worried about?" he said.

"You know damn well what I'm worried about," I said.

"You think once I get my hands on the notebook, I'll throw you to the wolves. Is that it?"

"In words of one syllable," I said. "Yes."

"You know me better than that," he said.

I grinned at him. Even he must have seen the funny side of that remark.

"I could throw you to the wolves anyway," he said. "My wolves."

I knew about his wolves. I had thrown people to them myself.

"But you wouldn't do that," I said.

"Don't bet on it," he said.

There was a pause before I spoke again. I made it sound casual.

"How much was Alworthy going to sell it for?" I asked.

Max shrugged.

"It's a fluctuating market," he said. "Something worth fifty thousand today is worth nothing tomorrow."

"Today's price," I said.

"To the Chinese, fifty thousand," he said reluctantly.

"That's a lot of money," I said.

"You're a long time dead," said Max. "Anyway, a commodity only acquires value if you know where the market is."

"I know," I said.

I had the satisfaction of seeing him look surprised.

"They've made contact with you?"

"No," I said. "You have."

He got the point.

"You're offering to sell it to me."

"Half price," I said. "With that much money I could take a trip where I wouldn't have to worry whether you did the dirt on me with Diaman."

"I wouldn't do that John. I gave you my word," he said.

I didn't labour the point. I let him sit there and sweat it out while the computer he carries around in his head worked out the permutations.

"What exactly do you want?" he said finally.

"Twenty-five thousand pounds, a passport, and your solemn promise that the Diaman business stays as it is, with me off the hook."

He pretended to consider it. Finally, he nodded.

"I agree," he said. He stood up.

"You'll make the arrangements?" he said.

"I'll make the arrangements."

I allowed him to shake my hand. He did so vigorously.

"Good old John," he said. "You always did manage to land on your feet."

He walked to the door.

"You won't let me down, will you?" he said.

"Don't you trust me, Max?" I said.

He smiled.

"Ofcourse I do," he said. "I'll wait to hear from you."

"You do that," I said, and showed him out.

I changed my suit and went to the office. There I tried to locate Danielle. I telephoned a couple of friends she used to have when we were married. They were surprised to hear from me, but no, they didn't know where Danielle was. Wherever she went after she left my office, she wasn't advertising it.

I took from my pocket one of the notebooks I had made up in the post office last night. I flipped through the pages quickly. Assuming the code that Dunning had used was a good one, it would take some time before anyone realised that what I had written was so much gibberish. I stuck the

note-book in an envelope and addressed it to Max. Then I
wrote a little note.

> Dear Max,
>
> Have the passport and the money sent Poste Restante
> to Bloomsbury Street Post Office in the name of Harper.
> I shall pick it up tomorrow morning. I'd like to say that it
> was nice to see you again, but it wasn't.

I signed it, and put it in the envelope with the notebook. Then
I called Miss Roberts in. I told her to walk to Leicester Square
Post Office and be sure to post it in the outside letter box marked
LONDON. NUMBERED POSTAL DISTRICTS ONLY. She put on her
fur coat, which didn't smell today, and left the office. The post
box was emptied every hour on the hour. At that time, any mail
addressed to United Rubber Estates Ltd., P.O.B. 17168, London.
E.C., was separated from the ordinary mail and taken by special
messenger to the Service building. I calculated that Miss Roberts
would post the letter in time for the two o'clock collection. Allow
another fifteen minutes for it to reach the Service and another
five for it to find its way up to Max. Give him ten minutes to
make up his mind that I was a complete idiot, and then either
make a phone call or not make one. By three o'clock, I should
know one way or the other. I looked at my watch. It was five minutes to two, so I had plenty of time.

As I left the office, there was a busty young hopeful waiting to see Stubbs. She switched on a smile when she saw me,
hoping to impress. But when she realized, I wasn't the man she
had come to see, she switched it off again. I felt like telling her
about Stubbs, but instead I left her to her illusions. That's all
she had.

I cashed a cheque for seventy pounds and left the bank
quickly before the manager could catch my eye. Two minutes
later, I was in Cecil Gee's, and the cashmere overcoat was mine.

I walked back to the office feeling ten feet tall. Miss Roberts had returned and I allowed her to take my coat from me. Her eyes widened when she felt the material. "Ooh, Mr. Smith," she said.

I smiled at her grandly and patted her bottom as I walked through to my own office. She blushed furiously, loving it, and rushed to pour me some tea. It was now ten minutes to three. I sat back in my chair and put my feet on the desk.

At three o'clock on the nose, Diaman loomed large in the door of my office. He looked like a man who had lost a penny and found a thousand pounds. There was a plain-clothes sergeant with him, but it was Diaman's moment, and he intended to enjoy it.

"John Smith, I have a warrant for your arrest that you did on the night of September twelfth feloniously..." He went on and on, a truly happy man, while poor Miss Roberts stood petrified in the outer office, her eyes growing wider and wider.

Good old Max, I thought. How could I ever have doubted his double-crossing, twisted little mind. He had made his phone call, and at last I knew exactly where I stood.

CHAPTER FOUR

I F the strings Max had pulled before had been slender and fragile, the ones he had to manipulate now were like steel hawsers, all snags and rough edges. I had been charged and the whole business had now become documented and official.

I was in the same cell as before when Max came to see me. He was livid.

"You've pushed your luck too far this time," he said. "I can't help you."

"You'll manage," I said.

"Some of the big wheels want you to swing," he said. "I don't blame them."

"You don't go along with them though."

"What a bloody fool thing to do," he said. "Have you any idea how difficult it is going to be to get you out?"

"That's your problem," I said. "You got me in."

"Christ!" he said. "I could cut your throat."

He was in trouble, and he knew that I knew it.

"I'm liable to get chopped for this," he said.

"That's the best news I've heard this week," I said. He was on his own hook. I wasn't going to help him off it.

He swore and he blustered for another ten minutes, stewing in his own juices. He had to get down to business sooner or later, and I wasn't going anywhere so I could afford to wait.

Finally, he cooled down a little. He squirted his eyes savagely, blew his nose and got down to the purpose of his visit.

"We'll arrange a transfer in Switzerland," he said.

"France," I said. He agreed.

"The notebook from you, twenty-five thousand pounds in dollar notes and a passport from us."

"Fifty thousand," I said.

He went red, then white, then red again.

"You agreed twenty-five," he said.

"You agreed not to sick Diaman on to me," I said. "We both made a mistake."

"I'll have to get it authorised. It'll take time."

"I'm not going anywhere," I said.

We blocked out the basics in ten minutes. He agreed to everything I said. He had to. Just before he left, he had one further thing to say.

"It'll take about a week to get you out," he said.

I grinned at him.

"Take as long as you like," I said. "But you won't find it."

He snarled at me and banged on the door to be let out.

"And, Max," I said. "Leave my girlfriend alone. If I find you've been round there again, it's all off." He started to look innocent, then decided that it wasn't worth it.

"I don't know where you intend going afterwards," he said. "But make sure that it's a long way."

"It will be," I said. "See you in court."

And that was the next place I did see him. I had been charged, so a court appearance was necessary. Somehow, they managed to get the preliminary hearing in camera. I stood in the dock and watched Diaman being slaughtered by the solicitor that Max had arranged. I had an alibi as strong as a twenty-foot wall and equally insurmountable. Not only was I not at the scene of the crime, but I had been seen by twenty people, including a bishop and a chief constable, two hundred miles away. I didn't get the full gist of it, but I think I was addressing a political meeting on behalf of the Liberal party. Diaman knew what was happening, and he bled to death quietly in the witness box. I felt sorry for him. He was in way over his head and the way out wasn't easy for him to take. He was a good policeman, and the foundation stone of his beliefs was taking a severe belting.

I saw him just before I left the court without a stain on my character. He had been severely criticised by the presiding magistrate for misusing his authority, and he looked like a fifteen-stone schoolboy leaving the headmaster's study after a beating.

"If it's any consolation to you," I said, "I didn't kill Dunning."

He looked at me sadly. He couldn't even find it in him to be angry at me any longer.

"Son," he said, "you can go out right now and cut the throat of anyone you want to. If I see you, I'll look the other way."

He lumbered off unhappily.

I saw Max, too, after the hearing. But we made no attempt to communicate with each other. Everything we needed to say to each other had been said. The transfer had been worked out, and as far as I was concerned, I didn't have to come in direct contact with him ever again.

When I got home my ticket to Nice was waiting in my letter box.

Vindictive to the end, Max had booked me on a night tourist flight for the following evening. I telephoned a travel agent I'd had dealings with and booked a first-class ticket out on the morning Air France flight. Then I phoned Phil Bannister.

"Want to go to Nice, Phil?" I said.

"When?"

"Tomorrow night."

"How much?"

"Fifty quid plus expenses and you can stay as long as you like."

"You're on," he said.

I gave him a few minor instructions, then put the ticket Max had sent me in an envelope and addressed it to his home. He'd probably stay there a week, drooling over the birds in their bikinis. But I owed him a favour. He had done odd jobs for me before. He was a good friend, close mouthed and reliable.

I packed a suitcase and at eight o'clock I called Mary.

"Alone?" I said.

"Hello, darling," she said.

"Food?"

"Lovely."

"Nine o'clock," I said, and hung up.

I posted the ticket to Phil on my way to pick up Mary, and we went on to have a ball.

Halfway through the most expensive meal I'd ever bought her, she started asking questions.

"You've won the pools?" she said.

"Nope," I said.

"Your maiden aunt has died?"

"Nope," I said, spooning another dollop of caviare into her avocado.

"I give in," she said.

I leered at her.

"When we get home," I said. "That's when you give in."

"I've got the curse," she said.

I must have looked shattered. She burst out laughing.

"I'm joking."

"It's nothing to laugh about," I said.

"It is from where I'm sitting. You looked like a little boy who'd had his lollipop taken away."

"I felt like one," I said.

Ten minutes later she approached the subject again.

"You've robbed a bank?" she said.

I shook my head.

"I know," she said. "You've done a Doctor Faustus. You've sold your soul to the devil."

This was the nearest she'd got so far. It was near enough to make me feel uncomfortable. She noticed my expression.

"I'm getting warm, aren't I?" she said. She put her hand on mine. "You haven't done anything stupid have you?"

I told her to forget about it and finish her meal. But the gloss had gone off the evening, and later at her apartment, the whole thing was a dead loss. I blamed it on the booze, and she was good hearted enough not to give me an argument.

I left her at two a.m. and drove down to see Gunther. During the night, it's easy to see if you're being followed, and if you are it's simple to switch off your lights and lay by long enough to lose your tail. I wasn't being followed. Max had obviously accepted the deal and was prepared to wait for the pay-off we had arranged.

I found the front door key over the lintel, and let myself in. I made no noise going up to Gunther's room as I didn't want to wake his daughter. I opened the door of his room quietly and found myself looking down the barrel of a Luger, held steady as a rock. For a man like Gunther old habits die hard.

He grinned when he recognised me and the gun disappeared.

"I nearly shot you," he said.

"You bloody old pirate," I said. "You're disappointed it wasn't someone you could shoot."

"At my age I would probably have missed," he said. "Have some coffee?"

I still didn't want to wake his daughter so I said no. But he had a thermos jug beside his bed and he poured a cup for each of us.

"So tell me," he said.

I told him exactly as it had been since I had last seen him. When I finished he was very quiet.

"What have I done wrong?" I said finally.

He shrugged his massive shoulders.

"Nothing," he said. "Everything you have done is fine. It is what you are going to do."

"The money." I said. It was a statement, not a question. He nodded.

"It is not good that you sell your country's secrets."

"I'm selling them *to* my country," I said.

"It is still not good." He shook his head. "I cannot understand this thing, John."

He rarely used my name. It was a sure sign that he was angry or upset. Then he noticed something in my expression and he started to grin.

"What are you grinning at?" I said.

"You called me a pirate," he said. "Next to you I am an amateur."

"I don't understand you," I said.

"How much is Max going to have to pay?" he said.

"I'm a very expensive investigator," I said. "Twenty-five pounds a day, all expenses, and a thousand-pound bonus because I nearly got killed.

"How much will all that come to?" he said.

"Including the time, I spent in prison, and the fortnight I shall spend in the South of France, about twenty-five days. First-class round transportation, and a suite at the Hotel du Golf at Valescure. Say two and a half thousand pounds."

He rumbled into laughter.

"What will you do with the other forty-seven and a half thousand," he said.

"Give it back to the Service," I said.

"Not to Max," he said.

"I shall pay it directly to Accounts," I said. "Max will have to explain why he requested a fifty-thousand pound payment for a two and a half thousand pound job."

"That is good," said Gunther, still chuckling. "That is very good."

"I knew you'd appreciate it," I said.

"And the poor policeman, he cannot touch you any more for Dunning?"

"No. The case was dismissed at a preliminary hearing. Max threw away all his trumps."

He grew serious suddenly.

"That is not like Max," he said.

"He had no alternative," I said. "He had to get me out."

But I had worried him.

"Even so, Max is not a man to release a hold once he has one. He got you out of prison before without it being necessary."

"I hadn't been charged," I said.

But he still didn't like it, and I began to feel uneasy too. Gunther could spot a rotten apple in any size of barrel.

"Let's go through it all once more," he said.

So we went through it. We went through it from the beginning, then we started at the end and worked our way backwards. We tried picking it up in the middle and working our way backwards and forward at the same time. We checked, we cross checked, and then we checked again. After an hour, one point stuck out like a sore thumb. Where was Danielle? She had started the whole thing off, then she had disappeared. Had it been coincidence that she had set me on to her husband on the very day he got himself killed, or was there something we hadn't seen? But if there was, we couldn't dig it out.

At half past seven, Gunther's daughter brought him his breakfast. If she was surprised to see me, she didn't show it. She went downstairs again and a few minutes later she returned with some breakfast for me. I left Gunther's at eight fifteen and drove straight to the airport. I parked my car and checked in. In the departure lounge, I joined the people who were fortunate enough to be able to take their holidays this late in the year. They were mostly eager young couples, and exhausted parents who had finally got their children back to school after having them home for ten weeks. They were now going away to recuperate.

Max was expecting me to leave by the night tourist flight, so there was no reason for him to have anyone at the airport this early. This evening, if he had decided to have me followed, the tail would pick up Phil Bannister and spend the next week following him around the low-life joints of the Côte d'Azur.

The flight was called and we trooped our way to the bus where we were jolted back and forth as the driver took us across tarmacs and under tunnels, to the waiting Caravelle. I took my seat on the port side of the plane, next to the window. After five minutes, we started to trundle to the take-off point. I accepted a barley sugar and a *Daily Telegraph* from the stewardess, and settled back to enjoy the trip.

The uneasiness that Gunther had instilled in me had evaporated somewhat during the drive to the airport. It still lurked sneakily at the back of my mind, but I had no intention of letting it spoil the holiday that Max was going to pay for. I hadn't flown for a couple of years and before that only twice since I had left the Service. The money I earned in my business didn't run to holidays abroad any more than it ran to cashmere overcoats. Now I had both, and I intended to get the maximum enjoyment from them.

I had four glasses of champagne on the journey. Champagne always tastes better on an aeroplane, probably because it's free. I read the paper briefly and then did the crossword. I'd finished the crossword by the time we swung east over Toulon to fly along the coast to Nice. The pilot announced St. Maxime and then St. Raphael on our left, and by the time he pointed out the town of Cannes we were well strapped in and sucking barley sugar again. As always at Nice airport, one got the impression one was going to land in the sea. Then the edge of the runway flashed past underneath and we touched down gently.

We were instructed to remain seated until the aircraft had completely stopped and we were informed that the outside temperature was fifteen degrees. I tried to work out quickly whether that was overcoat weather. But I can never remember whether one has to multiply by nine and divide by five, or the other way round, and whether one adds thirty-two after or before. I finally settled for looking out the window to see what the people outside were wearing. On the restaurant balcony it was shorts and open necked shirts, and I surmised that it wasn't overcoat weather.

We straggled our way across the tarmac and queued to have our passports looked at. Then we waited fifteen minutes for our baggage. I collected my one suitcase, cleared the perfunctory customs barrier, and went to hire a car.

Ten minutes later, I was seated at the wheel of a Renault and bowling along the coast road with the impeccable blue Mediterranean on my left. Before reaching the Autoroute d'Estorel, I stopped for some lunch. The first meal eaten in France is invariably the best. The fish was superb and the wine was cold and complimentary. I capped the meal with a large brandy, and returned to the car with all doubts and uncertainties long gone and forgotten.

The Golf Hotel at Valescure, as the name implies is well known to golfers and very few others. It sits alone in a pine forest five kilometres behind St. Raphael.

My suite was on the fifth floor, and from my balcony I could look out across the tops of the trees to St. Raphael and the coast. The trees themselves looked like a sea of rich green waves piling one on top of the other, broken here and there by outcrops of white rock, which were the villas built in the forest. It was quiet, peaceful, and ten thousand miles away from London and Max.

I spent the balance of the afternoon flat on my back by the side of the swimming pool, soaking up the sun whose August savagery had mellowed to September benevolence.

Later, I returned to my room, bathed and changed then wandered down to the bar. I drank four *pastis* while I relearned elementary French from the bartender. Then I strolled out to the terrace for an early dinner.

I ate fresh grilled sardines, and drank a bottle of St. Roseline, while I watched the mosquitoes fry themselves to death on the electrical traps dotted about the terrace. They would fly up, attracted by the blue neon tube, then hit the exposed wires and explode with a crack. I was feeling so good it didn't even spoil my dinner. I lingered over coffee, and at half past ten I drove back into Nice. I parked the car at the airport and went into the terminal building.

I was upstairs in the bar when the night tourist flight from London was announced. I finished my drink and walked along the first-floor balcony until I could see where the passengers came out after clearing customs. Phil was the fourth person to come through, lugging a suitcase and dressed for a Soho bottle party rather than the South of France. He turned right and came across to the news-stand right beneath where I was standing. They were just about to put up the shutters, but he managed to buy a packet of cigarettes, and he stood there while he opened the packet and lit one. But I wasn't watching him, I was watching the other passengers who followed him out. They were the ones who travelled by night flights, and who for the sake of saving a fiver or thereabouts are happy to start their holiday with a sleepless night and indigestion from eating airline sandwiches at one o'clock in the morning.

None of them followed Phil, and I was beginning to think Max was getting soft in his old age, when Phil decided he had accomplished what he had been told to do. He picked up his suitcase and started out of the building with that lecherous predatory look that all Englishmen adopt when they arrive in France. As he did so, a small bald-headed man who had been dozing on one of the couches, woke up suddenly and trotted after him.

I could almost see Max's expression back in London. The report would have come through that the man travelling on John Smith's ticket, wasn't John Smith. So, what the hell was John Smith up to? Follow the man anyway. A phone call would have been made to Nice and Phil's description passed. Now Phil had a tail until he decided that the fleshpots of Soho were better than the fleshpots of Nice, and went home. And until I made the contact I had arranged, Max would sit in a cold sweat in case I pulled the whole thing down around his ears. So, let him sweat, I was only returning a favour he'd done me on a hundred different occasions.

I motored back along the autoroute at a steady fifty, while the Mercs and the Thunderbirds streaked past me at more than a hundred. The guests of the Golf Hotel are early-to-bedders; they're due on the first tee at seven thirty in the morning. So the hotel was shut up tight when I got back and it took me fifteen minutes to raise the right porter. He came grumbling to the door to let me in. I bought a bottle of Evian water from him, and tipped him sufficiently for him to forgive me for waking him up. I went up to my room and there I slept for ten solid hours, to be awakened at midday by ecstatic shrieks from the direction of the swimming pool.

But today was a workday, the day I earned my pay. I shaved and dressed while I drank my coffee, then reluctantly leaving my new overcoat behind, I went downstairs. I handed in my key, and after stopping for some petrol, I drove through St. Raphael to Fréjus Plage.

A couple of hundred yards back from the coast road is a large apartment development. There are four unsightly blocks of flats spaced round a dreary patch of scrub which is supposed to be a garden. I parked the car outside the West block and went up to the fourth floor. There was no elevator and I was puffing like a grampus by the time I rang the doorbell. I decided to cut down on the booze and get more exercise. The door was opened by a pretty young girl of nineteen or thereabouts dressed in a white bikini, with a small apron tied round her waist. The overall effect was highly erotic. She smiled at me and asked me what I wanted. Before I had time to bring a blush to her cheeks, she was pushed out of the way by Gar Davies, who smothered me with enthusiasm. He was short, stocky, fifty-five years old, with the energy and appetites of a man of thirty. He had been born in Egypt of

British parents and lived there until he had been slung out by Nasser. He had tried to settle in England but decided the climate would kill him, so he had moved to the South of France. Using the compensation money the British Government had given him by way of an apology for allowing him to be slung out of Egypt, he had started a real estate business here in St. Raphael. He had prospered in spite of the heavy anti-British and anti-Semitic sentiments of his competitors.

The girl continued to float around in the background until he patted her backside and told her to go and sit in the kitchen. He spent ten minutes telling me what had happened to him since I had last seen him in England; then I gently pulled him back on the rails. "The notebook," I said.

Every Frenchman—and Gar was a Frenchman by inclination if not by nationality—keeps a safe in his home. The safe may only be a hole in the floorboards or a cashbox stuffed at the bottom of a dirty linen cupboard, but in it he keeps a few papers and a vast amount of ready cash for doing business. Seventy per cent of the business done in France is done in cash, which explains why France is one of the poorest countries occupied by the richest people in Europe.

Gar fetched his safe out. It was an old cashbox that could have been opened by a disinterested boy scout. From it he pulled something like twelve thousand pounds in five hundred-franc notes, and the notebook I had sent him.

Inside the cover of the notebook he had slipped a few sheets of paper, which were covered with his neat, spidery writing.

He spread the sheets of paper in front of me.

"This was a very difficult code at first," he said. "It was difficult because it was so simple. There was no key word. It took me four days to realise that. Afterwards it was still difficult. Every letter is represented by a group of symbols, and there is no means of judging how long each group is. I had to resort to trial and error."

"But you managed," I said.

He smiled and nodded.

"I will show you," he said.

He pointed out the first line in the notebook.

24XB379yrc47aab986YYbBV

"The first group is 24XB37," he said. "That represents the letter 'H'."

"How do you know?"

"I worked it out," he said, as though I was asking a stupid question. "The next group is 9yrc4," he said. "That is the letter 'O'. The next group is longer for no other reason than the man who made this up wanted it that way. It is 7aab986Y. That is the letter 'M'. The next group includes the last four symbols on the line, YbBV, and also the next two on the next line, but reading from right to left. The letter is 'I'. And so it goes on, group by group, line by line, reading first left to right, then right to left." He slammed his hand down on the notebook. "I had a lot of fun with this," he said. "It was like the old days."

During the war he had been the top cypher man in Middle East Intelligence, and bloody good at his job. If he told me he had broken down the contents of the notebook, it was good enough for me. He continued.

"The first word appeared to be HOMING, and I thought I was well on the way. But then it didn't make sense with what followed. I thought perhaps it was a code within a code, and that now I would have to break a second cypher." He looked up at me suddenly. "You would have saved me a lot of trouble if you had told me there was Chinese involvement," he said.

"I didn't know when I sent you the notebook," I said.

"When I realised it was so," he said. "It was easy. HOMING wasn't one word, it was two. Ho Ming, you see, a name. It is followed by an address and by a small piece of information about the man."

"What sort of information?" I asked.

"He is a senior clerk in the foreign bureau in Peking."

I thought about this for a while.

"The whole book is the same?"

Gar nodded.

"There are fifteen names and addresses, and similar pieces of information about each person."

"Nothing else?"

"Nothing."

He watched me for a moment.

"Is it what you expected?" he said.

I hadn't known what to expect. For fifty thousand pounds the merchandise had to be pretty substantial. I think I assumed it would be the plans of the latest cobalt bomb, or whatever it is they're making now. But these fifteen names were far more important. The life of a spy or an agent or whatever you want to call him, is a pretty lonely one. Even his friends are his enemies when it suits them. His only ally is his anonymity. Here we had the names of fifteen men, or women for all I knew, who were working and living in the Peoples' Republic of China, and whose anonymity was only a shade from being destroyed. It was no wonder that the Chinese would pay high for the list, and that Max would pay equally high to make sure they didn't get it. The Far East had not been one of my territories when I was in the Service, but I knew enough about it to know that reliable agents there didn't grow on trees. Apart from any other consideration, they had to be Chinese. An Englishman, if he was expert at languages, could pass as native in most European countries, but try to slip him into China and see how far he'd get. I thought for a moment about those fifteen Chinese, living day by day under the shadow of the executioner's sword, or whatever they use in China, and I decided that the sooner I got the notebook back to Max, the better.

I thanked Gar and together we burned the papers he had worked on in solving the cypher. I declined the invitation to lunch, and left after promising to come and see him again soon. The girl in the kitchen saw me leaving and bounced to her feet in anticipation. Gar still didn't introduce me, so I contented myself with a leer, and left as she started to remove her apron.

Outside I lifted the engine cowling on the car and removed the battery. I put the notebook on the battery stand, and replaced the battery on top of it, screwing it firmly back into place. I put the phony notebook Max had thrown at me the last time I saw him into the glove compartment. Even now, I didn't trust him. I wanted my hands on that fifty thousand pounds before I turned over the goods. I know I was going to turn most of it back to the Service, but what with cashmere overcoats and jaunts to the South of France, my expenses were way over the top, and I had no intention of winding up out of pocket.

As I pulled away from the apartments, Gar waved to me from the balcony. There was a flash of white and brown behind him, and he disappeared inside. He had the sexual appetite of a pasha, and I had kept him busy for quite long enough. I still had two hours before making the rendezvous but I wanted to spy out the land first. Once before, when Max had thought he had got the notebook, he had shown that I was expendable, and I wouldn't have put it past him to send a couple of the Heavy Squad to take delivery, with instructions to see that I met with a fatal accident at the same time.

I knew what it was like getting money out of the Service treasurer, and the thought of paying out fifty thousand pounds must have been like a kick in the crotch to Max. He'd be no end of the fair-headed boy if he could do the job and not have to pay out.

There would be no sure way of knowing whether the men I met were Heavy Squad men. It had been five years since I'd been in the Service, and in that time most of the personnel would have changed. The mortality rate was the highest of any squad in the Service. It was for this reason that I had chosen this particular rendezvous. I would be able to see a false move for two miles in either direction, and would be able to act accordingly.

The autoroute that connects Fréjus to Nice has been carved through the hills behind the coast on the premise that the shortest distance between two points is a straight line. It dips and curves in places, but in general it is like a great wide ribbon, loosely meandering between those two points without a single curve that can't be taken at a speed of a hundred miles an hour.

In places it is paralleled by sections of the old road, and in other places a bridge carries a less exalted road across the top of it. If you leave the autoroute at La Napoule, just before Cannes, and then double back for twelve miles, you find one of these bridges. This I did, parking my car off the bridge, out of sight. Then I walked out on to the bridge and looked down at the autoroute beneath me. I could see two miles towards Fréjus, and two and a half miles towards Cannes. Nobody was going to sneak up on me from either direction.

The road which the bridge carried was a different proposition. It wound down through the hills, crossed the autoroute, then climbed again the other side. But here I was banking on ignorance to keep me out of trouble. My instructions to Max had been simple and explicit. The rendezvous was to be on the autoroute exactly thirty-two kilometres from the Fréjus toll both. The man making the contact was to move on to the hard shoulder of the road when his milometer told him he had covered that distance. He was to wait for me there. I had made no mention of bridges, and I trusted Max's enthusiasm would override his natural caution, and that he would not have such a thing checked. If things worked out, I would make the transfer and then return to my own car and drive off. The man or men on the autoroute would be trapped there, unable to find an exit for the next fifteen kilometres, by which time I would be long gone.

It was a good, simple plan, one which enabled me to investigate who I was meeting before I actually met them, and which gave me an unbeatable start should they feel inclined to follow me. The fact that the whole thing turned into such a shambles had nothing to do with me; it was still a good scheme. There was an hour to go before my contact could be expected, so I returned to the car, removed my shirt and started to soak up some sun. But there is a difference between the sun that bathes you by the side of a swimming pool, and the sun that broils you when you're surrounded by acres of rock and scrub. Yesterday by the pool had been fine, here after twenty minutes I was sweating like a pig, and there was no way to cool off. I put my shirt on again and immediately it was soaking. So I sat in the car and roasted out the next half an hour while the sweat on my shirt grew cool and clammy. Ten minutes before time, I took the phony notebook from the glove compartment, slipped it into my hip pocket, and walked back towards the bridge. It was a little before four, an hour when the French are usually finishing their lunch, so there was very little traffic about. What there was zoomed past beneath me at speeds of seventy-five and above.

I spotted my man when he was still a mile away. He was in a small, three-year-old Simca, pottering towards me at a steady thirty miles an hour. I moved down off the bridge to a point where I could see and not be seen. As the car approached the point of contact, the engine started to cough, and a moment later the car moved over to the hard shoulder, and the engine conked out altogether. I didn't know what the men were going to be like, but the car was a bloody good actor.

There were two men, and they both got out. I didn't recognise either of them, but that wasn't surprising. One was about forty-five, and looked as though he had seen it all and didn't much like any of it. I could feel for him. The other was younger, about twenty-five or six. The older man stood close to the car, while the young one opened up the engine cowling and looked inside. He wasn't as good an actor as the car had been. They looked genuine enough; the older was too old to be a Heavy Squad man, and as the Squad always travelled in pairs, it was safe to assume the young one wasn't either.

I climbed out of the ditch and walked on to the hard shoulder about fifty yards away from them. As he saw me the younger man jumped as though he had been scalded. Max was scraping the barrel with that one. The older man didn't even blink. He reached into the car and when he straightened up again he was holding a black leather wallet about eight inches long and three inches thick. That one wasn't going to part with what he was holding until he had the notebook, he was too old a hand. As I reached him, he spoke to the younger man without turning his head.

"In the car," he said.

The younger man looked as though he'd have liked to give him an argument, but he didn't. He slammed the hood shut and got into the passenger seat.

The older man allowed his eyes to flicker past me, taking in the bridge and what it implied.

"Clever," he said. Then he looked back at me. "Do you want to count it?" he said.

"Just see it," I said.

He lifted the flap of the wallet and I saw the bundles of used dollar and sterling bills. I held out my hand for it, but he shook his head.

"After," he said.

"I'll get it," I said. I turned away.

"It's in your pocket," he said. He could see it sticking out of my hip pocket.

I took it out and flipped it to him. He caught it with one hand, opened it and looked at the first line that was written there. Then he looked up at me and nearly smiled.

"I'll wait," he said.

I walked back to the point where I had come on to the road. I was about to slither down the embankment when something I heard suddenly struck a jarring note. I looked back towards the car, the man standing beside it, and the autoroute beyond. In the minute we had been standing there, a couple of cars had passed us, and we hadn't even noticed them. There was another car coming towards us now, a large white Mercedes, and I realised what had made me turn. A quarter of a mile away the driver had changed down. There was no reason to change down, unless it was to stop, and there was no reason to stop.

The older man had noticed it too, he was looking back over his shoulder towards the approaching car. He said something I couldn't hear to the younger man, who started to get out of the Simca. He didn't make it. The Mercedes swept on to the hard shoulder still doing forty although the brakes were now hard on. It slammed into the back of the Simca, knocking it fifty yards up the road almost to where I was standing. I could see the younger man inside, as he was slammed backwards over the front seat, and then, as the Simca hit the side support of the bridge, stopping dead, he was pitched back to the front of the car again, his head and shoulders smashing through the windscreen.

The older man was still going for his gun when they shot him. Two men leapt from the back of the Mercedes, which had now stopped and ran back to where the older man was lying like a bundle of old rags. They picked up the wallet and the notebook from beside the body, then they jumped back into the Mercedes which had reversed to pick them up. There was a clash of gears and the Mercedes swung off the hard shoulder and was doing sixty before I could catch my breath. The whole thing had taken less than thirty seconds. From where I was standing, I could see a pool of blood seeping out from beneath the bundle of rags that was the older man. The younger man's head was still sticking through the windscreen, but I decided I wasn't going to do any-one any good by hanging around any longer.

I slithered down the bank and ran across to my car. I couldn't find the bloody key for a moment, then I remembered I had left it in my jacket pocket which I had taken off and thrown into the back. I found it and started the car, turning it so that I would be able to go back the way I had come. I'd started to sweat again, only this time it wasn't the heat. I hadn't got a very good look at the two men from the Mercedes, but good enough to see that one of them was Chinese.

CHAPTER FIVE

IT's surprising the number of Asians who live and work among us. They're so much part of the pattern that we don't notice them, that is until we're looking. Now it seemed that every third person I saw hailed from the East. They probably came from Japan, Thailand, Cambodia or Malaysia. But to me they all looked Chinese, and they all looked dangerous.

I was in a blue funk. After the autoroute incident, I drove up into the hills behind the old coast road and found a small restaurant that looked as though it hadn't had a client for the past twenty years. I parked the car well out of sight from the road, went in, and ordered a large vodka. They didn't have any vodka, but it was the end I was after, not the means, so I had a large brandy instead.

I was way up the creek without a paddle, and I didn't know what the hell I was going to do next. One thing was certain, I had to get the notebook back to Max as soon as possible. What is more, I had to advertise the fact that I no longer had it in my possession. It would take the Chinese no time at all to see that they had hijacked the wrong notebook. After all, they must already know the code. When they realised it, they would be after me like a modern day bunch of Genghis Khans.

The Chinese may be behind the West in matter of science and technology, but they have nothing to learn when it comes to spying and other miscellaneous thuggery. They had agents at work when the British were still painting themselves blue, and the only real American was the Red Indian. And that popular supposition about Asians being the most patient people on earth is so much eyewash. They can be as impatient as the next man when they want something really badly. And their means of obtaining it don't bear contemplation; they were the inventors of painful persuasion.

As far as I was concerned, the airport was out. So too, were the main-line stations. I could try driving across the border to Italy and catching a plane from Genoa, but they'd probably be watching the border as well. That left me one way out. Drive north, making for Paris, and pick up a plane there. They would be watching the main roads, the *Routes Nationales* 7 and 85, so I would have to do it by easy stages, sticking to the back roads. I didn't doubt for a moment that they knew what I looked like. If their organisation was efficient enough to have discovered my rendezvous with the Service, it was efficient enough for anything. For that reason, I couldn't go back to my hotel. I could see my new cashmere overcoat hanging in the wardrobe where I had left it but, as a measure of how scared I was, it didn't seem important any more. My hide would keep me warm enough, and if I went back to the hotel, I stood a good chance of losing that, too.

I finished my drink, had another, and then decided that I couldn't delay the decision any longer. I borrowed a touring map from the proprietor, and worked out a torturous route taking in Draguignan, Comps, Digne, then branching on to the RN 75 at Sisteron. I decided I would make my first stop at Rives, after by-passing Grenoble. I would plan the second stage of the journey from there.

It was dark by the time I left the restaurant. Going from the warmth and light of the small bar, into the anonymous darkness outside, took quite an effort, and I nearly succumbed to the proprietor's insistence that I stay for dinner. But I didn't. I settled instead for a couple of sandwiches and a bottle of wine which I took with me.

I passed over the bridge that I had left in such a hurry a couple of hours earlier. The wreckage of the Simca had been pulled well to the side, and I wondered if either of the two Service men were now resting in hospital, or in the morgue.

I cut across country to Draguignan and headed north through the wide beautiful country towards Comps. Not that I could see the country; it was dark. If it could have stayed that way for the next week, I would have been happy.

I made bad time at first, due to the number of times I stopped to make sure I wasn't being followed. Each time I picked up headlamps in my rearview mirror, I'd kill my own lights and coast into a layby. There I would wait in fear and trembling until the car behind me had passed. After Draguignan, I stopped doing this for each car that crept up behind me, and although it gave me a few uneasy moments, I made much better time. By midnight, I was past Sisteron and halfway towards Grenoble. I arrived at Rives at four in the morning, and the small town was closed up as tight as a drum. I parked off the road near a bar which looked as though it might open early, and tried to snatch a couple of hours sleep in the back of the car.

At six a.m., I saw someone moving about inside the bar, so I knocked on the door and was let in reluctantly. While the coffee was being made, I phoned Gar and asked him to wait a couple of days then collect my things from the Golf Hotel and send them to me in London. I just hoped I'd be there to receive them. Gar's nose for such things scented some excitement, and I almost told him to come and join me. But selfish as I sometimes am, I'm not that selfish. I finished by telling him I was in trouble with some girl and that I had to slip away unobtrusively. This he understood, and he promised to do what I asked.

By seven, I was on the road again. I reached the outskirts of Paris just as it was getting dark. I was nearly at the airport when I had a better idea. I swung west around Paris and picked up the RN 1 towards Calais. I would spend the night in a hotel I knew at Montreuil, and then drive into Le Touquet first thing in the morning. I could leave the car at Le Touquet and pick up the first plane to Lydd. The fact that I had virtually stolen the car, and that the hire firm would have no trouble in tracing me, didn't enter my calculations. Indeed, the thought of being safely locked away in jail, even a French jail, was quite intriguing. The other side of St. Germain, I stopped long enough to phone ahead and book my room. I had a couple of stiff drinks and then settled down to the last stage of my drive.

I arrived at Montreuil just after nine and drove straight to the Hotel Château de Montreuil. When the receptionist realised that I had no luggage, he had a quiet word with the manager. Full of *bonhomie,* the manager told me to leave my car keys with him and he would see that the car was washed for me. I didn't want anyone fiddling with the car, but as he had no intention of having it washed, I left them with him.

The dining-room was nearly empty as I had my dinner, and I went to my room immediately afterwards. I had a terrible night, dozing on and off. Each time I dropped off, my dreams were full of Fu Manchu-type characters chuckling among themselves because I thought I had escaped their oriental clutches.

I went downstairs at six thirty and borrowed a razor from the night porter. Half an hour later, I left and drove the twenty minutes to Le Touquet airport. There was a plane due out at eight o'clock so I bought a one-way passenger ticket, and then parked the car at the far side of the car park where it would probably stay for days before anyone noticed it.

I went back into the airport building and tried to get some breakfast to stay down. The airport was quiet at that hour in the morning. Trim young ladies in uniform were opening up the various enquiry and ticket desks, chattering among themselves in French and English. A captain who looked as though he should be in charge of a VC 10 and not just a Bristol Freighter, passed the time of day with a nubile looking wench who was supposed to be opening the perfume counter. It was all very ordinary and very peaceful, and for the first time since the autoroute business yesterday, I began to feel easier. I ordered another coffee and a brandy to help it down. The first plane over from England had arrived half an hour earlier and the English newspapers were on the news-stand. It wasn't until I went to buy one that I realised it was Sunday. I bought the *Sunday Times,* and moved over to the lounge to wait for my flight to be called. I could see two cars being readied for the plane, while their accompanying passengers were spending the last of their francs at the gift shop. I was halfway through the Colour Supplement, trying to locate the editorial content from the advertising, when I heard my name called on the public address system. "Mr. John Smith to the British United enquiry desk please." I started towards the desk, and I saw the girl who had sold me my ticket earlier point me out to a uniformed young man. He thanked her and headed across towards me.

"Mr. Smith?" he said as he reached me.

I nodded.

"If you want your car loaded, sir, you'd better hurry," he said politely.

That meant that somebody had seen me arrive by car.

"I'm not taking it," I said.

"In that case may I suggest that you lock it, sir? You've left it unlocked and the keys are still in the ignition." I thanked him, and feeling that I could cheerfully cut his throat, I started towards the exit doors. But he was full of good intentions, and was determined to follow it right through. He fell into step beside me. He talked as we walked.

"Lucky for you, sir, I noticed it," he said. "We try to take care of the cars that are left here, but we do like the owners to meet us halfway by taking normal precautions. It would be comparatively simple for someone to get in your car and just drive it off. Ofcourse, he wouldn't have the papers, but ..."

"Yes, he would," I said. "I left them in the glove compartment."

He was so bloody pompous and self righteous that I wanted to deflate him. He wasn't deflated, just superior. He talked to me as though I were a complete bloody fool.

"That's a very careless thing to do, sir."

"Yes, isn't it," I said, striding out across the car park to where I had parked the car in the mistaken impression it wouldn't be noticed.

They must have been waiting on the other side of the car park. As I reached in to take out the keys, I saw through the windscreen, an old black Citroen suddenly stop broadside on in front of my car. The only occupant was a cloth capped driver.

I pulled back out of my car so fast I hit my head a crack on the top of the door frame. My hand went involuntarily to my head to nurse the bump, and I turned to the pompous young man for protection. Even *they* wouldn't do anything foolish with a witness present. But the pompous young man had gone. At least he was still there, but he wasn't the same man. He didn't even look the same. It was the gun that did it. It was held steadily, pointing at my middle. Now he gestured towards the Citroen with it, and still nursing my head I did what was expected of me. I walked the six feet to the Citroen as the driver leaned back and opened the rear door. I got in, and the uniformed young man got in beside me. As he settled back, he removed his peaked cap and I realised that he wasn't wearing a uniform at all, but a well-cut navy blue suit. Put an ordinary chauffeur's cap on top of that and you've got a uniform, especially in an airport when every second person seems to wear one.

But that was the least of my problems. As the car pulled round in a wide circle and swept out of the airport gates, I made myself as small as possible in the corner of the seat and prepared to meet my doom.

Like a lot of people, I have a low tolerance to pain. Even a visit to the dentist is something of a traumatic shock, and my dentist isn't particularly painful. Let someone threaten to extract my fingernails one by one, or shove a red hot poker up my backside, then that someone can have from me, everything that his heart desires. In other words, I'm a coward. I have been told by people who are supposed to know me, that I have the faculty for covering up this fact, burying it beneath a stiff upper lip and an air of bravado. But I have never been aware of this fact and, if it is so, it is due no doubt to my belief that the person threatening me wouldn't actually carry out his threat. It takes courage of a different sort to physically torture another person, and the people I had dealt with in the Service were mostly as frightened as I was. But old-fashioned torture is not used much nowadays. There are so many medical ways to extract information that it has become obsolete like the bow and arrow and the atom bomb. A quick clean jab with a hypodermic is far less trouble than a pair of hot pincers. Under a truth drug, a man can be made to tell everything he knows, and there is the added attraction that what he tells is the absolute truth and not some fabrication screwed out of him by pain.

This was the general trend of my thinking as I sat in the back of the car. They were certainly going to sweat it out of me, and I hoped desperately that they were civilised enough to do it in a civilised manner. As an added bonus to not suffering any pain, one had the consolation that even the strongest man couldn't have resisted. This provided a salve to the conscience afterwards. If there was to be an afterwards. I looked sideways at the young man sitting next to me. He was staring at me, his gun loosely held on his lap. But it wasn't a stare of curiosity, it was the stare of a professional who knows that the only way to watch a man is to do just that. In fact, there was a complete disinterest in his gaze. If I suddenly sprouted another head, he wouldn't bat an eyelid. His only concern was that this particular bundle he had picked up didn't do anything stupid like trying to get away.

How they had found me I didn't even begin to consider. I learned later that they had checked at my hotel, and when I hadn't returned, they had simply put a man on every airport in the country. Don't ever let anyone tell you that the Chinese aren't well organised. Not that either of my two companions were Chinese, they were as French as the Eiffel Tower. They were hoods, plain and simple. Sixty-two per cent of the world's illegal drug supplies comes from Communist China, and if you are the principal suppliers to the French underworld of such a commodity and you ask for a little favour to be done, your wish is treated as a command. The two in the car were merely messengers. They were delivering a package without any knowledge of the contents. We went out of Le Touquet over the bridge at Etaples and swung left on to the coast road towards Boulogne. Ten miles after Etaples, we passed through a small village. The man sitting with me grunted something to the driver, who nodded. We stopped on the far side of the village.

As the man sitting with me got out of the car, the driver turned in the front seat so he could watch me. He, too, had a gun which he levelled at me across the top of the seat.

In the rearview mirror, I could see the first man walk back up the road into the village. He turned into a shop which announced by a sign that it contained a public telephone. Three minutes later he came out again, walked back to the car, and we were on our way once more.

At one time during the drive, I considered whether or not to appeal to these men's patriotism. After all, France was in this Western Alliance thing as much as Britain, however much de Gaulle argued to the contrary. It was Napoleon himself who said "Let China sleep, for when she awakens, the whole world will tremble." But hoods have no nationality, and without nationality there can be no patriotism.

We were two hours in the car, and during that time not one word was spoken. So I had plenty of time for thought, and I thought plenty. The principal thing that occupied my mind was that the notebook, which I was obviously supposed to provide, was still resting secure beneath the battery in the Renault at Le Touquet airport.

We turned off before Boulogne, and my visions of a slow cattle boat to China receded somewhat. Then forty miles beyond God knows where, we turned into the gates of an old château. At the back of my mind, habits of a lifetime had assimilated the directions we had taken, and I knew I could find the château again blindfolded. That, in itself, was ominous. It pre-supposed that they didn't care what I knew about them, because the knowing wasn't going to do them any harm. The only reason they could assume that was by assuming that I would be dead.

We pulled up in front of the crumbling façade of the château, which looked like something out of Charles Addams. If any money had been spent on the place during the last twenty-five years, it must have been on the cellars. It certainly didn't show above the ground. There were cracks an inch-wide meandering down the walls. Some of the shutters hung drunkenly, others had given it up entirely and fallen to the ground. These had left great holes in the walls where the stonework had rotted and crumbled around the rusty bolts that were supposed to hold them in position.

The grass, on what I assumed was once a lawn, stood knee high, and somewhere in that jungle there must have been a pool of some sort because the whole place smelled of long-stagnant water. Even the sun, which had been doing its best all morning, realised that it had met its match here. It had disappeared behind a large black cloud, and obviously had no intention of appearing again.

The driver got out and opened the rear door for me. In the moment when the man with the gun was off guard, getting out of the car behind me, the driver took his place. They were obviously under the illusion that, given the slightest chance, I would run. I had already run seven hundred miles and it had got me nowhere. There didn't seem much point in running again, especially as there was nowhere to run to. I walked up the wide front steps, nearly breaking a leg on a cracked piece of paving stone. The driver pushed open the door and we all went in.

The interior of the château fitted the exterior well. It was like an old, old man who had long ago realised that he was about to die, and in consequence had decided that nothing mattered anymore; no need to wash, or clean his teeth, no need to dress, or even get up. Just lie still while the barnacles grew and death crept down. It had been elegant once, the wide sweep of the staircase and the double height of the hall showed that. At the far end of the hall were huge windows, the glass miraculously intact, which looked out on to a sloping vista of land which still bore traces of the formal garden it had once been. Beyond lay twenty miles of hazy countryside.

I was steered to the left of the hall, through a pair of double doors into what had once been the drawing-room. There was an ornate Louis Quinze fireplace complete with chipped marble cherubs, and the remains of a huge gilt framed mirror above it. Like the hall, there was no furniture.

I started across the room towards a door at the far side, assuming it was expected of me. Then halfway across the drawing-room I was prodded gently in the back with the gun and told to stop. I didn't turn for a moment, wondering if I was going to get it now, and not wanting to see it coming. Finally, when I did turn, my two companions were already walking out of the door to the hall again. They left without so much as an "au revoir".

I was still standing there with egg on my face when I heard a car start up outside. I moved over to one of the front windows in time to see the back of the Citroen as it disappeared down the drive. Then the sound of footsteps from the hall pulled me round. I debated whether to make a dash for the far door, but

I was far too intrigued by now. Instead, I crossed the room and went out into the hall to meet whoever it was I could hear.

There was a tall, thin man coming down the stairs. He was brushing some dust off the sleeve of his jacket. He smiled at me like an old friend.

"Mr. Smith isn't it?" he said.

I nodded.

"Fascinating place," he said. "It must have been quite beautiful once upon a time."

His accent was barely noticeable, and certainly insufficient from which to judge his antecedents. His suit was a charcoal grey shantung, his shirt and tie silk. He looked like one of those "men of distinction" advertisements, and as out of place as Dracula in a creche.

He reached the bottom of the stairs and stood looking at me for a moment, still smiling.

"I must apologise for meeting you here," he said. "It doesn't belong to me; it was loaned to me by a friend."

"The same friend who loaned you those two men who just left?" I asked.

"Exactly," he said. "You're very observant. But then observance has always been a strong point of yours hasn't it?"

"Has it?" I said.

"Don't be modest, Mr. Smith. Rio, seven years ago."

I *had* been in Rio seven years ago. Something to do with an ex-Nazi who had offered us something in exchange for saving him from the Jews. What he was offering hadn't been of much value, but I had accepted it anyway, and then told the Jews where to find him. It had been a bit of a balls-up from start to finish, but somehow I had come out of it well, and even Max had congratulated me.

"I don't remember you," I said.

"I wasn't there," he said. "But I read the reports on the case. Very impressive."

"Whose reports?"

"Mine," he said.

"You don't look Chinese," I said, fishing desperately.

"Albanian," he said. "Although I do spend a great deal of time in China of course."

"Of course," I said.

"But how rude of me," he said suddenly. "I haven't introduced myself."

He stuck out his hand.

"My name is Igor," he said.

I was obviously supposed to shake his hand, so I did. His handclasp was dry and surprisingly strong for so lean a man.

"Just Igor?" I said.

"Just Igor."

I was playing for time now, sorting through the card index in my mind, looking for an Igor. But it was five years out of date, and any filing system falls flat after that length of time.

"I hope you'll excuse the manner in which I had you brought here," he said. "But I had to see you before you returned to England. If I hadn't known better, I'd have thought you were trying to avoid me."

"Why should I want to do that?"

"That's exactly what I said to myself," he said. "Come."

He started towards the glass doors at the end of the hall. I followed him.

The catch on the doors was rusted beyond recall, and after fiddling with it for a moment, he stood back and kicked at it with the bottom of his shoe. The doors flew open, letting in a gust of fresh air, which made me realise how dank and musty the château was.

"We'll walk in the garden," he said.

If that was what he wanted, who was I to stop him? I followed him out on to the terrace, and at that moment the sun decided to come out again.

It was very pleasant in the garden. We walked, and we talked. We sat for a while on an old stone bench and we talked some more, the château looming in the background. It was all very civilised and I wondered when the crunch was going to come.

"I followed your exploits with interest," he said. "You were a highly successful operator. We couldn't understand it when you dropped out of sight—six years ago, wasn't it?"

"Five," I said.

"We thought you had gone underground," he said. "You had us worried for a time. But then we found you again and we realised what had happened."

"What?"

"Disillusionment," he said. "The occupational hazard of our profession. We look beneath the flag-waving and the patriotic slogans, and what do we find? We find that we are in the dirtiest business of all, doing nasty little jobs for very little money."

He was no fool. He knew what he was talking about.

"After a couple of years, we marked your file closed and that seemed to be that."

He looked at me suddenly. His eyes were grey and vaguely glassy. I decided that he wore contact lenses.

"Why did you decide to come back?" he asked.

"You know why," I said, hoping desperately that he would come up with an answer that I could tag on to.

He continued to stare at me for a moment, then he nodded.

"Yes, of course," he said. "'Tis a consummation devoutly to be wished.'"

So he quoted Shakespeare. I wasn't impressed.

"What is?" I asked.

"Financial independence. Opting out of the rat race. I'd have done the same thing in your place."

He was beginning to lose me, but I didn't want it to show.

"It's not unusual," I said.

"No, it's not, and I commend you for it," he said. "The question is, where do we go from here?"

I waited for him to tell me.

"You are a seller in a seller's market," he said finally. "That's always a strong position."

"The strongest," I said.

"I am one of the buyers for what you wish to sell. The other is your man what's-his-name."

He knew bloody well what his name was.

"Max," I said.

"That's him, Max," he said. "Max was willing to pay you fifty thousand pounds-worth of dollars for it. I can be more generous, I'll give you seventy-five."

"That's not being more generous," I said. "You've already got fifty thousand of it from Max."

"But I *do* have it," he said. "And I am prepared to add twenty-five thousand more. I couldn't be fairer than that, could I?"

"What about the passport?"

"That, too," he said. "But I give you fair warning. You cheated Max. You sold him a counterfeit. I will not be so treated. Before I pay you the money, I shall want to be absolutely sure that I am buying the genuine thing."

"If I allow you to open the merchandise and check its authenticity, there'll be no need for you to pay me the money," I said.

"Then we must devise a scheme where both our interests are guaranteed," he said.

"What do you suggest?" I asked.

"I suggest we arrange a rendezvous. I come alone with the money, you come alone with the notebook. It will take me five minutes to authenticate the contents. If I am satisfied, we can both leave together and go our separate ways."

Stated like that it sounded very simple, but there were holes in it large enough to drive a horse and cart through.

"Who chooses the rendezvous?" I said.

He shrugged.

"It doesn't matter," he said. "As long as we both agree."

That seemed fair enough, and I said so.

"Paris?" he suggested.

"London," I said.

"Why London? I should have thought you wanted to stay well away from Max's clutches."

"The best way to stay out of Max's clutches is to get so close to him he can't see you," I said. "Besides, that's where the merchandise is."

He thought about this for a moment, then he nodded.

"Very well," he said. "London."

We started to walk back towards the château.

"Your Max would have been very angry if we hadn't interrupted your transaction yesterday," he said.

"I shouldn't think he's over-delighted about it even now," I said.

"A hijacking he can understand," he said. "It's an occupational hazard. But to have carried through with the transaction and paid out the money in good faith only to find that you had cheated him—that would have been far worse."

There wasn't much I could say to this, so I said nothing.

"I presume you intended contacting us eventually," he said.

"Of course," I said.

"And selling us false information too?"

"Probably," I said.

"Extremely clever," he said. "You would have been in possession of a permanent pension. Every time you needed more money you could have played us off against each other."

I decided that we'd gone far enough into the realms of fantasy, and I started looking for a few answers.

"How did you get on to Dunning in the first place?" I asked.

He didn't seem to mind.

"Dunning approached us through diplomatic channels," he said. "We, of course, were extremely interested."

"So was Alworthy," I said.

"Naturally," said Igor. "I wonder what happened to him."

"I killed him," I said, trying not to sound like Humphrey Bogart.

"I imagined you had," said Igor. "For a man who had so much at stake, he behaved extraordinarily foolishly."

"Yes, didn't he," I said, wondering what the hell he was talking about. Then he allowed me to slip off the hook.

"Tell me, how did *you* get on to Dunning?"

"Connections," I said.

"Through your ex-wife I suppose."

"Exactly," I said. I was groping around in the pitch dark and any moment I was going to say the wrong thing. But once more he steered the conversation away from the edge.

"You are a patient man," he said. "I admire you for it, To wait as long as five years before moving in for the big kill requires self-control of the highest order."

"There was no point in moving in for a kill that wasn't big," I said.

"Tell me," he said. "When your nose for such things detected what was afoot, did you realise that the pay-off would be so high?"

"Of course," I said grandly. "It needs all of fifty thousand to assume a new identity in comfort."

"And now you have seventy-five thousand."

"That's the difference between comfort and luxury."

"Where will you go?"

"South America," I said.

"Very sensible," he said.

We reached the terrace and I was about to go in through the french windows when he redirected me.

"My car is round the side," he said. "I'll drive you back to the airport."

We walked along the terrace and round to the side of the château. Parked close to the wall was a large grey Rolls with Italian number plates. Sitting behind the wheel was a Chinese chauffeur.

He got out of the car as we approached and opened the rear door for us. I got in first, and Igor behind me. As I settled back in the comfortable smell of real leather, the chauffeur got back behind the wheel and started the engine. Or rather, I assumed he started the engine. I couldn't hear anything.

Igor lowered the partition window and told him to drive to Le Touquet airport. Then as the car purred off towards the château gates, he raised the partition again and sat back with a little sigh that denoted that as far as he was concerned, all was right with the world.

"Things must be looking up in Albania," I said, looking round the interior of the car. Igor pulled a face.

"It's a terrible country," he said.

"You must make a splash when you drive up to party headquarters in this," I said.

"I don't take the car to Albania," he said. "When I am there, I use a bicycle. Fortunately, I am not there very often."

I tried to visualise him cycling along the road with all the other good little Communists. I couldn't get the picture at all.

"The Party are very lenient in the matter of expenses." he said. "As long as the results are satisfactory, their tolerance is unbounded."

"You should try working for Max," I told him.

"He's an interesting person, your Max," he said. "He possesses an unusually devious mind for an Englishman."

I suppose you could have called Max devious, I preferred to call him pig-headed and mean.

"This whole business worried me a little at first," he said. "There were an extraordinary number of loose ends which I didn't like. Not least was the fact that the admirable organisation Max runs hadn't started to suspect Dunning far earlier."

This had worried me too, but I let it go.

"Then I heard that Alworthy had moved in and I worried even more," he went on. "He had the homosexual's nose for intrigue, which was why he made such a formidable opponent."

"He was an idiot," I said.

"Yes, wasn't he. Still, it is through such idiots that people like you and I can work. When he failed to get hold of the notebook, I thought Max had located it and I was prepared to see the whole thing go out of the window. Then came your arrest and that extraordinary farce Max was forced to arrange in the English courts. I knew then that you must have something he wanted very badly."

He was very well informed, and I told him so. He shrugged it away as something of no particular importance, and took no credit for it. I almost began to like him at this point.

A couple of miles further on, he got down to business.

"How long do you need to set up the rendezvous?" he said.

"Two days."

"Where will it be?"

"I'll contact you," I said. He gave me a London number through which he could be passed a message.

"I shall be in Paris," he said. "When I hear from my contact, I will come over to London. Allow me eight hours from the time you make the call."

I memorised the London number and then lapsed into silence. I now had to work out how I was going to get the notebook out of the Renault without his being aware of it. There was a possibility he would remain at the airport until my plane had left and I didn't want to have the complication of coming back for it. Neither could I afford to let him know of its existence on this side of the channel. If he did, he'd have it off me so quickly I wouldn't be able to duck the bullet he would give me in exchange. Likeable as he was, he was still a professional and would cut me down like a piece of grass if it suited his purpose.

This problem occupied me for most of the journey, and I was still no nearer a solution when we reached the airport.

It was just past mid-day, and the airport was busy. The car park was full of cars waiting to take their places on the outgoing flights and becoming tangled up with those which were arriving on the incoming ones. Their passengers milled about in family groups with the lost look that most people have at airports.

We drove straight to the main entrance and the chauffeur got out to open the door for me.

"I'll wait to hear from you," said Igor.

"I'll be in touch," I told him.

At least he wasn't going to hang around until I boarded the plane. It was a help, but not much.

As we had driven into the airport, one thing had struck me immediately and with considerable force. In spite of the general confusion, with cars going every which way, it stuck out like a sore thumb. The Renault had disappeared.

CHAPTER SIX

I WATCHED the Rolls sweep imperiously from the airport on its way to Paris. No doubt Igor would stop at the first telephone and arrange for someone to pick me up at Lydd airport. He had got his hooks into me and he wasn't likely to let go. I didn't doubt that he was prepared to pay the promised seventy-five thousand pounds, but only as a last resort. For the next few days, until I fixed the rendezvous, I would have to be prepared for a tail that would stick like glue. But that was the least of my problems. The vanishing Renault had first priority. Without the car, there was no notebook, and without the notebook, I was as low on the totem pole as it is possible to be.

I started with the RAC. No, they knew nothing about it. Why not try the police? Next I tried the AA. No, why not try the police? I tried the airport manager's office. No, better try the gendarmerie. All roads seemed to lead to Rome so, much as I hated the idea, I went to the police. They had an office at the airport and I was shown into a room where I was kept waiting for twenty minutes while they looked for Monsieur l'Inspecteur.

They found him in the middle of his lunch. As he came into the office he was buckling on his belt and looking livid.

"How can all this bloody nonsense about a missing motor car be important enough to interrupt my lunch?" That isn't exactly what he said, but that's what he meant. I explained to him how I had left the car and how when I had returned it had gone.

"How long were you away?"

"Four hours or thereabouts," I said.

He called in a sergeant and ordered that a call be put out to watch for the car.

"The number?" he said, turning to me.

"I don't know," I said.

"It is on the papers," he said.

"I don't have the papers," I said.

"Where are they?"

"In the car."

I was forced to go on to tell him that just so it didn't inconvenience the thief too much, I'd left the keys in the ignition as well.

His red face became even redder, and realising that he could say 'au revoir' to his lunch, he got down to business.

"The car is yours?"

"No, it belongs to a hire firm in Nice."

"In Nice?" he said. "Do they know their automobile is a thousand kilometres from home?"

No, they didn't, I said. He booked a call to Nice, explaining that I would have to pay for it. Then, while we were waiting for the call to come through, he started on another tack.

"You say you purchased a ticket on the eight o'clock plane. Why didn't you take it?"

"Something came up," I said.

"You only purchased a passenger ticket. What were you going to do about the car?"

"Leave it here," I said.

"You told the owners in Nice of course?"

"No, I didn't," I said.

And so it went on, with me putting my foot in my mouth every time I opened it. I believe he almost began to welcome being called away from his lunch. As far as he was concerned, the case had started to develop interesting sidelines that lifted it above the level of a mundane car theft. The call to Nice came through and, as I was paying, the inspector took his time. He asked about the weather on the coast, and remarked how he envied those who lived there all the year. He reported on the weather here in Le Touquet, and finally, after five minutes, he condescended to get down to business. Yes, Mr. John Smith had hired a car from them. No, they didn't know Mr. Smith was going to drive to Le Touquet and abandon it, and if it had been stolen, they would inform the insurance company, knowing meanwhile that Monsieur l'Inspecteur would use all the forces at his command to retrieve it for them. *Au revoir* and *bonne santé.*

There was a further hour of questions before the inspector grew tired of the whole thing. He apologised that there was nothing he could charge me with and suggested I wait around the airport until he had some news. Then he left abruptly, presumably for his tea.

I didn't feel much like hanging around the airport, so I left a number with the sergeant and took a taxi into the town. I walked into the Hotel Westminster and as I was telling the receptionist that I might be getting a call from the police, the call came through.

They had found my car abandoned in the forest, about two miles from the airport. It had been driven off the road into the trees. Would I please go and identify it. They said they didn't have any transport to spare so would I take a taxi. They gave me the directions and I had a taxi drive me out. Funds were running pretty low by this time, and if somebody at British United wasn't going to be broad-minded enough to take this morning's plane ticket in exchange for a new one, I could see myself spending the rest of my days in Le Touquet. The taxi driver had some trouble in finding the spot and, when he did, there was one bored constable waiting for me.

All the seats had been taken out of the car and the floor covering stripped off. Apart from that, it was the worst bit of searching I'd ever come across. I can only assume that the men Igor used were more used to looking for five-pound boxes of heroin than they were for slim thirty-five page notebooks. Which only goes to show that a man should stick to the trade he knows and only employ experts in the same trade to do his odd jobs for him. If they'd even bothered to lift the engine cowling, it didn't show. I identified the car for the constable and offered to drive him back to the airport. He accepted with alacrity, and after putting the seats back we drove to the airport, where I dropped him off. I then drove to the far side of the car park and under the guise of fiddling with the engine. I removed the notebook from beneath the battery. I collected the car papers, locked the car carefully and went back to the police office in the airport building. Fortunately, the inspector wasn't there. I phoned the hire firm at Nice and arranged for them to pick up the car. Then I left the keys and the papers with the sergeant and went to see British United. They were extremely helpful and changed my early morning ticket for one out on the next flight. At two-thirty I was on my way.

The journey takes twenty minutes, and I was at Lydd and through customs and immigration by three o'clock. The customs officer looked at me a little strangely when he realised that not only did I have nothing to declare, but I actually had nothing at all. Still, they can't pinch a man for travelling without luggage and, after waving his bit of chalk around, wondering what he could mark, he passed me through.

As I had expected, there was a tail waiting for me. He was a youngish man with a sickly white pallor which looked as though it had never seen the light of day. He was quite good, inasmuch as he didn't jump a mile when he saw me, but he was so out of place at the airport that I spotted him long before he saw me. Knowing he was going to be with me for the next couple of days I christened him for ease of reference. I called him Horace.

On the plane, I had started a conversation with a returning holiday family named Cummings. There was forty-year-old father, thirty-year-old mother, and three children whose ages were indeterminate. Father was so glad to find someone to talk to after having the family around his neck for the past fortnight, that he offered me a lift into London. This had been my point in starting the conversation, and I had accepted gratefully. In the car park, mother and the children were shoved into the back of the car with the luggage, and I was given the seat of honour next to the driver. As we drove out of the airport, I saw Horace get into a Vauxhall to start earning his pay.

Cummings turned out to be one of those drivers who feel the public highway is their own private road, and that nobody else has any right to be on it at all. Within ten minutes of leaving the airport, I was regretting the whole thing. The family must have been used to it. They chattered away happily in the back, while I quietly died in the front. Horace, I'm sure, had thought he was on to an easy pitch following a family saloon, and the fact that he managed to keep up with us at all sent him up in my estimation. We reached the outskirts of London at five thirty and twenty minutes later, I said good bye to the Cummings family. My right leg was as stiff as a board from applying a non-existent brake for the past sixty miles. How I had avoided shoving my whole leg through the floor of the car was a miracle.

About now, Horace became a little confused. Following a car had been all right, but now I was on foot and he was still in his car. Added to this, Cummings had dropped me near Victoria, and Horace wasn't going to be able to find anywhere to park. I watched him drive past where I was standing, frantically looking for a hole where he could tuck his car. I allowed him to drive past me, then I crossed the road and caught a bus going in the opposite direction. Half a mile down the road, I got out of the bus and went into a tube station where I bought a ticket to Piccadilly Circus.

At Piccadilly, I fought my way out against the down-pouring commuters. In the concourse, I rented a left luggage locker, and I locked the notebook in it. Getting rid of it was like discarding a ball and chain. The thin book had weighed a ton in my pocket. I went to the public toilet and paid the appropriate fee for the privilege of taking a crap, and I dropped the key of the locker into the water cistern. Then I went home.

Horace was parked fifty yards down the road in his Vauxhall. He must have been very relieved to see me. I resisted the impulse to wave at him, and I let myself in. The flat, which is pretty crummy at the best of times, felt and smelled as if it hadn't been occupied for a decade. But however it felt and smelled, it had nothing on me. I'd been in the same clothes since leaving the hotel in Valescure two days before. Since then, I'd sweated on the autoroute, driven seven hundred and fifty miles, spent a terrible night in Montreuil, sweated some more when I was picked up by Igor's men and sweated some more under the influence of Cummings' driving. My shirt was so stiff I practically broke it taking it off and I smelled like an old gymnasium. I poured myself a massive drink and took it to the bath with me.

I lay in the bath for two hours, freshening it periodically by turning on the tap with my right foot while removing the plug with my left. During that two hours I did some very hard thinking. By the time I got out of the bath, I was as red as a pillar box, and my skin had crumpled so that it looked as though it didn't fit me any more. But my thinking bout had served its purpose. I now had the whole thing neatly set in order and analysed. I'd judged every move since the whole mess had started. The conclusion was final and absolute. I was still in it up to my armpits, with even less chance of coming out of it than I had had before.

I know I had the notebook. And all I had to do was to take it to Max. But then Igor would be after me and I'd seen enough of him to know that once he got his teeth into something he'd not let go until he'd shaken the life out of it. It would be useless to ask Max for protection. Once he got the notebook back, Max would do the necessary to me—but quick. On the other hand, I couldn't let Igor have the notebook either. I'm pretty stupid most of the time, and this was one of those times. Even for seventy-five thousand pounds I couldn't allow those fifteen Chinese names in the book to go for the long chop. But if I didn't contact Igor by the day after tomorrow, he was going to contact me. And this time it wasn't going to be a polite discussion in an elegant old château, it was going to be a noisy killing in a dark and dirty alley.

After I clambered out of the bath, stupefied with the booze and the heat of the water, I came into the bedroom and started across to the wardrobe with the intention of getting my dressing-gown. I sat on the bed for a moment to scratch my stomach, and one thing led to another. The pillows looked very comfortable, and I liked the feel of the mattress beneath me. I lifted my legs on to the bed and stretched out experimentally. The moment my head hit the pillow, I died.

I must have been in the same position when the Heavy Squad arrived three hours later. I was conscious first of a very bright light obtruding into my sleep. Then, before I could identify or even be fully aware of it, somebody clouted me on the side of the head, and I rolled off the bed. Still stark naked I was jerked to my feet, with a hand under each arm. A man is at his most vulnerable when he's wearing no clothes, added to which I was still half asleep and didn't know what the hell was happening. I stood, supported on each side, my mouth hanging open, trying to organise some sense out of the chaos. I was helped in this direction as I received another clout round the head, and was dropped into the bedroom chair. I started to get out of the chair and was pulled back by four large hands from behind. Then, from the shadows, a towel was thrown at me.

"Cover yourself up, you look revolting," said Max.

I draped the towel primly across my lap as Max stepped into the light. When Max is feeling benevolent, he's a formidable character. When he's feeling mean, one is hard put to find any comparative depth of meanness. At the moment he was obviously feeling just as mean as he could.

He had a thin, tight, smile pinned on, which fooled no one, least of all me.

"Been having yourself quite a little jaunt," he said. I said nothing. When the Heavy Squad hit you, you knew you had been hit, and the bells hadn't yet stopped clanging.

"How much did you take them for?" said Max.

Rather stupidly, I told Max to go fornicate with himself and immediately received another clout which practically took my ear off. Max just stood there, his hands stuffed deep in his coat pockets, looking mean.

"How much?" he said.

"Nothing," I said. I braced myself to lose the other ear but nothing happened.

Max fetched an upright chair and carried it over towards me. He sat on it back to front, his face fourteen inches from mine. I could see that his conjunctivitis was giving him hell and I could have spat straight in his eye if I'd had any spit. But my mouth felt as though it were stuffed with dusty carpet.

"Marchesson was a good operator," said Max.

Marchesson must have been the one who was shot on the autoroute. If I hadn't known Max, I would have thought his anger was due to the shooting of Marchesson. But I did know him, and I knew that Marchesson could have been hung, drawn and quartered in Max's living-room, and he wouldn't have batted an eyelid. It was the money that was sticking in his gullet, and the fact that he'd lost the notebook. He would look on happily while twenty Marchessons were killed if he could rectify either.

"Try looking to your own bloody security," I said. "Our meeting place was blown."

"You're a liar," he said.

"So I'm a liar," I said.

I saw Max shake his head quickly, and I realised I had narrowly avoided being thumped again.

"If the rendezvous was blown," said Max. "You blew it."

"I suppose I killed Marchesson, too," I said.

"I wouldn't put it past you," said Max.

I said a rude word, and when the expected blow didn't come, I started to regain some of my confidence. Not much of it, but sufficient to ask if I could put something on. It was cold and I was beginning to shiver. Max nodded his agreement.

As I put my dressing-gown on, I saw the two Heavy Squad men for the first time. They were large and anonymous. I didn't know either of them. They stood behind the chair I had just left with a hawk-eyed indifference. One wrong move and they would have knocked my head off. When I'd done up my dressing-gown I sat on the bed. If I was going to be hit again it would have to be from the front.

"If they got what they wanted, why were you picked up at Le Touquet?" said Max.

"If you knew I was picked up at Le Touquet, why didn't you stop them?" I said.

Max brushed this away indifferently.

"They had the notebook. What did they want with you?"

"Perhaps they didn't like the notebook they had," I said.

Max's eyes flickered briefly like one of those panels on a computer as it digests a problem and hasn't yet pumped out the solution.

"They haven't got it?" he asked.

"Right," I said.

He expelled his breath slowly. Then he looked up at the two Heavy Squad men.

"You can go," he said.

They left quietly and unobtrusively, without a backward glance.

"What happened?" said Max.

I told him about the abortive meeting on the autoroute, and the opposition's departure with the wrong notebook and the fifty thousand pounds.

"What about Le Touquet?" he said.

I told him. At the mention of Igor's name, he sat up a little.

"Igor Berat?" he asked.

"Just Igor as far as I'm concerned," I said.

"It must be Berat," he said, half to himself.

"Should I know him?"

He looked up at me as though he had forgotten about me. Then he shook his head.

"No. He's only been around for four years. And very long years they've been."

"Big wheel?"

"You could say that. What was his proposition?"

"Your fifty thousand and twenty-five more."

"You agreed, of course."

"I agreed," I said.

"So why didn't you let him have it while you were still in France. What made you come back to London?"

"I found out what was in the notebook," I said.

This didn't impress Max.

"So?" he said. As far as he was concerned it might have been a grocery list in the notebook. People don't rate very high in Max's scheme of things.

"So if fifteen people are going to get the chop, I'm not going to wield the axe," I said.

"Not even for seventy-five thousand pounds?" He couldn't believe that anyone could be so stupid. Then he had an idea. "You think I'm going to offer you more?"

I let him get on with it for a while. It's fascinating sometimes to watch a snake screw himself up.

"What kind of a bastard are you?" he said. I could see he regretted having dismissed the Heavy Squad. "You'd sell out your own mother if the price was right. We made a deal—fifty thousand pounds for the notebook. I've come up with the fifty thousand pounds and by Christ I'm going to get the book in exchange."

"I've been offered seventy-five," I reminded him.

"I don't care if they offered you the Great Wall of China. By Christ, I'm going to turn you over to the Heavy Squad with a black ticket." He was already halfway to the telephone when I stopped him. He was practically rigid with anger and his eyes had started to stream. He must have gone over the top to have even thought of turning me over with a black ticket. The colour codes for the Heavy Squad were white, which meant a little roughing up with not too many bones broken: grey was designed to be used on people who were reluctant to divulge information needed by the Service and was always very painful. The only people who were issued with black tickets were those who were going to die alone in some far away place where their dying inconvenienced no one, least of all Max.

"It's not for sale anymore," I said as he reached for the phone. He'd worked himself into such a pitch that I wondered if I'd got through to him. He had the phone halfway to his ear when he started to relax. He put the phone down again, and fumbling in his pocket he produced his eye drops. He squirted them into his already streaming eyes, and then mopped up the deluge with his handkerchief.

Then he came and sat on the bed beside me. I got up and moved to the chair.

"What do you want?" he asked.

"All I want from you is enough to cover my expenses," I said.

"And?" said Max. He knew me.

"And twenty-four hour protection until Berat decides to stop chasing me."

"He's not chasing you."

"He will be as soon as he realises I'm not going through with it."

"Where do you keep the booze," said Max suddenly.

He followed me into the living-room where I poured two drinks. I handed him his and watched while he walked over to the window and looked out into the street.

"You're being followed," he said.

"I know."

"Shall I have him removed?"

I shrugged. It didn't make much difference. I wasn't trying to hide. Not yet, anyway. Then he turned from the window, his mind made up.

"We'll kill two birds with one stone," he said. "You get Berat over here. You get the money from him and turn back to me my fifty thousand. You can keep half the balance."

"There won't be any money unless I give him the notebook."

"Give it to him," said Max. "We'll pick him up immediately afterwards. I've got a lot to talk over with Mr. Berat. It should be very interesting."

"It's risky," I said. "What if you don't pick him up? He's got the notebook."

"We'll be sitting on his head two minutes after you hand it over," he said. "The meeting place is your choice. We'll find a place we can button up so tight that no one will get away."

"Not even me?" I asked.

"That's a nasty thing to say," said Max.

"I've got a nasty mind," I said.

He didn't give me any arguments.

"You'll have to trust me as much as I'm going to have to trust you," he said.

This was a pretty poor arrangement, but there wasn't much I could do about it. I told him so.

"Good," he said. "I'll contact you when I've sorted out a suitable meeting place."

He headed for the door, then he turned back.

"How much is 'enough to cover your expenses'?" he asked.

"It doesn't matter anymore," I said. "I'm going to get half of twenty-five thousand."

He looked at me steadily for a moment. His eyes were dry now.

"Nevertheless, what do you consider your services over the past few days have been worth?"

"Why?"

"I'm curious," he said.

"Two and a half thousand," I said, naming the sum I always intended to keep.

"As much as that," he said. "I'm obviously in the wrong business."

"We're both in the wrong business," I said.

"You should be happy. You're going to get a very large fee and do a bit of good at the same time."

"Good for whom?"

"Your country," he said. I laughed in his face. He looked as though he wanted to say something but bit it off short, and he left.

He was right, ofcourse. I should have been happy. I would get paid. I'd get shot of the notebook and Max would take Igor off my neck. So why wasn't I happy? There was a little crawling creature lurking around inside my head. I couldn't pin him down and the harder I tried, the deeper he crawled. There was something wrong somewhere. And I didn't have any idea what it was.

After Max had left, I considered going down to Box Hill to see Gunther. But I'm a big boy now, I thought, and I must learn to stand on my own two feet. Apart from that, Horace was still outside, and while I didn't doubt my ability to lose him again, I could have been wrong, and there didn't seem any point in taking the chance of dragging the Old Man into it.

It was still only just after midnight, and I was wide awake now, I thought about calling Mary, but decided I wouldn't do her the unkindness of wishing myself on her in my present state of mind. Instead, I cooked myself some bacon and eggs. The bacon had been in the fridge for over a week and was a little tired round the edges. But it tasted all right. I made myself a pot of coffee and started to think about things. Somewhere along the line I fell asleep.

On my way out at nine thirty the following morning, I saw that Horace's place had been taken by another man. He was using the same car, sitting low in the driver's seat, with a newspaper held up in front of him. He gave me fifty yards start, then he got out of the car and started following me. He was cut from the same mold as Horace. He could have been his brother. I called him Wallace.

Miss Roberts was ecstatic when I walked into the office. It had been two weeks since she had seen me, and what with the appearance of the police just before my disappearance, she had begun to doubt that she would ever lay eyes on me again. She fussed around like a mother hen, bringing me three cups of tea in the first five minutes. She gave me a quick rundown on what Stubbs had been up to, which turned out to be exactly nothing. Then she brought me my mail. There were three circulars, seven assorted bills, and a postcard from Phil Bannister in the South of France. In it he said he was having a ball, and he knew I wouldn't mind if he stayed over for a further week. I'd forgotten about Phil. That was another item for my expense sheet. There was also a printed form from Her Majesty's Customs and Excise saying they were holding a suitcase at London Airport, addressed to me. Would I please go and collect it? So I hadn't lost my overcoat after all.

Miss Roberts also gave me a list of telephone messages, none of which meant anything, except the last name on the list. Mrs. Robert Helix had called. Barbara Helix had been one of Danielle's friends I had telephoned when I was looking for her. I was still looking for her, so I called Barbara and identified myself.

"Would you like to take me out to lunch?" she said.

I said that I wouldn't, and what did she want.

"I'm not sure I'll tell you if you don't take me out to lunch."

"I can take you to the Corner House," I told her.

"I was thinking of the Caprice," she said.

"You can think again," I said. "I can't afford it."

"Well, I'm not going to the Corner House," said Barbara. "Not that I don't think it's very good," she added. Her husband had once been a Labour M.P. and, as much as it went against the grain, Barbara tried to help him with his image.

"Does that mean you won't tell me?" I enquired.

She told me, as I had known she would. It seemed that a couple of days after I had phoned enquiring for news about Danielle, Marjorie Adams, another mutual friend, had returned from Madrid where, she reported, she had seen Danielle.

"So there you are," said Barbara. "She's in Madrid—or at least she was."

I thanked her and was about to hang up when she continued:

"Don't you want to know who she was with?" she said.

I didn't, but I asked nevertheless.

"Michael Lumsden," she said, like he was the Aga Khan.

I said, "Oh really!" or something equally fatuous, but she wasn't going to let go.

"He's that terrible man who was married to Katherine Lumsden. All four of them used to go around together when they were married."

"When who was married?" I said.

"All of them. Nathaniel and Danielle, Michael and Katherine."

I knew Dunning's death had been kept out of the papers, so I dug a little.

"You mean Michael and Katherine are divorced now?" I said.

"Of course," she said. "They all got divorced about the same time."

"All of them," I said.

"Nat and Danielle, Michael and Katherine. You knew, surely."

I said I didn't.

"No reason why you should really," admitted Barbara. "It was all very quiet and discreet."

"How long ago did all this happen?" I asked.

"Two years. No, two and a half. I remember because Danielle asked if she could use the cottage while she was waiting for her decree thing, and she couldn't because I was there getting over an abortion."

I thanked her politely, and hung up.

I thought of Danielle's clothes I had found in Dunning's bedroom, of her make-up and perfumery laid out on the dressing-table. And I thought of the place where I had found the notebook, in Danielle's secret hiding place. There was a mistake somewhere, and Barbara must have made it.

I sent Miss Roberts down to Somerset House. Because it was urgent, I told her to take a taxi there and back. She was back inside the hour. And there it was, in black and white. My ex-wife had asked me to obtain evidence so that she could divorce a husband she hadn't been married to for over two years. Whichever way you sliced it, Danielle had set me up and led me to the chopping block.

I was still trying to work out the whys and wherefores when Miss Roberts buzzed me on the phone.

"There's a gentleman to speak to you," she said. "He won't give his name."

A lot of my clients are like that, and I didn't want to be bothered with clients right now. I told Miss Roberts so, and she buzzed me back thirty seconds later.

"He says his name is Oxford," she said.

Oxford had been a name I'd occasionally used when I had been working for Max. I asked for him to be put through, at the same time telling Miss Roberts to bring me another cup of tea. She would listen happily at the switchboard for hours if I didn't do something about it.

It was Max.

"Can you come and see me?" he said.

"Don't forget I'm tailed," I said.

"I'll take care of it," he said. "Leave your office at exactly twelve forty-five. I'll expect you at one."

As I left the office at twelve forty-five, a young lady was hitting Wallace about the head with her handbag, and screaming that he'd made indecent advances towards her. Two policemen were ambling over the horizon, and as they moved in on either side of Wallace, engulfing him, I hailed a taxi. Then, in case Wallace had seen the number of the taxi, I paid it off around the corner, and walked the rest of the way.

Max must have been feeling very pleased with himself. He got to his feet as I was shown into the office, and even came round the desk to pull up a chair for me.

"Sit down, John," he said. I sat.

"Cigarette?" he offered. I took one.

"It's all laid on," he said.

"What is?" I said.

"The meeting place for you and Berat. We've got to play it very cool. Berat is expecting you to come alone, so we'll stay well out of sight until after the transaction. Then we'll pick him up."

"What happens if he decides he's not going to part with the money and tries to pay me in kind?"

Max looked at me fondly.

"There'll only be the two of you," he said.

I remembered the surprising strength of Igor's handshake, but I nodded.

"What happens after you pick him up?"

"You give me the money, after the deductions, and go on your merry way."

"No repercussions?"

"None."

I thought about it for a moment. There didn't seem to be any way I could get out of it, so I agreed.

"Where's it to be?" I asked.

"Psychologically, the place has to be dead right. It has to be a place that Berat would expect you to choose if you were meeting him alone. A place where neither you nor he can call up the cavalry at the last moment."

"Where is this place?" I said.

"If it's not dead right, he'll smell a rat and won't turn up at all."

"Where is it?"

"It took a little thought, but ..."

"Stop flannelling me, Max," I said. "Just tell me where the bloody place is."

He looked mean for a moment, then he shrugged it off. He reached into his centre drawer and pulled out a map. He turned it so that it faced me and stuck his finger on a point about twenty-five miles east of London. I leaned forward and removed his finger so that I could see what he was pointing at.

"You're kidding!" I said.

"It's an ideal place," he said.

I got to my feet.

"What's the matter with it?" he said.

"It stinks, and you know it."

His mouth tightened up and his eyes started to water.

"Any better ideas?"

"Dozens. And so have you. What are you up to, Max?"

He started to bluster with his number two indignant expression. I'd seen it before and I wasn't impressed.

"I don't like your choice of rendezvous," I said. "What's more I don't like anything about the whole bit."

He stopped blustering and grinned at me.

"So, what are you going to do about it?" he said.

There was nothing I could do about it and he knew it. I sat down again and he got down to business, showing me exactly where and how I should meet Berat, and where and how the Service were going to pull him in afterwards. He had all the details worked out meticulously. Every move was plotted and counter-plotted. But I still wasn't impressed. To my way of thinking, the whole thing had assumed melodramatic proportions quite out of keeping with the essential simplicity of the operation. And the operation *was* simple. If one forgot for the moment the ramifications built into the notebook, the whole operation boiled down to a simple exchange—notebook for money. It was the sort of thing that could be done in an Oxford Street cafe in two minutes flat. Yet Max detailed to me a plan which was complicated enough to have been used for the Great Train Robbery.

I left the office an hour later with one thought uppermost. Max was up to something sneaky. And when Max got sneaky, someone usually got hurt. It didn't take three guesses to know who that someone was liable to be. I went straight back to my own office. There was no sign of Wallace. He was probably languishing in Saville Row police station by now, waiting for the magistrate to sit next morning. I spent ten minutes trying to locate Marjorie Adams's number, and finally got her on the line.

"Yes," she said. "I saw Danielle in Madrid."

"Any idea which hotel she was staying at?"

"Why?"

"I want to contact her."

"I know that, but why?" she said.

I spun her a yarn about a second cousin in from the colonies who wanted to see her. I thought for a moment that she wasn't going to bite. She relented finally.

"The Hilton," she said. I thanked her and hung up. I should have guessed. If there was a Hilton hotel, Danielle would be in it. She had an affinity for the streamlined, super-efficient, completely impersonal atmosphere Mr. Hilton has scattered across the globe. In a Hilton hotel she knew she could drink the tap water, and she knew that the cooking wouldn't be foreign if she didn't want it that way and the beds would be without bugs. She was a little like a Hilton hotel herself, streamlined, efficient and impersonal.

I asked Miss Roberts to place a personal call to Mrs. Dunning at the Castellana Hilton in Madrid. Then I remembered that she wasn't Mrs. Dunning any longer. It was no good trying to work out what name she was now living under, so I took a chance and asked for the call to be made to Mrs. Lumsden. If she was staying with the man in Madrid, there was a fair chance that she would be using his name, if only to keep the hotel management happy.

The call came through an hour later.

"Danielle?" I said.

"Who is it?"

"John."

"John who?" she said. After three years of being married to me, she had to ask that.

"John Smith," I said.

There was a moment's pause.

"Hello darling," she said. "How are you?"

"I want to talk to you," I said.

Considering I had bothered to phone her clear across a continent, it was a pretty fatuous remark. But it didn't make any difference, as it was the last thing I had a chance to say.

"Darling, this is a terrible line, I can't hear a thing," she said. I could hear her as clearly as though she were in the next room. I started to say so, but she didn't let me finish.

"It's no good, darling, can't hear you. I'll be back next week. I'll call you then." And she hung up.

The English operator asked me if I had finished because my party had cleared. I said I hadn't and asked to be reconnected. Then something went wrong with the lines between here and Madrid and it was half an hour before I got through to the hotel again. I was told that Mr. and Mrs. Lumsden had checked out ten minutes ago and left no forwarding address.

CHAPTER SEVEN

THE street was the same, with the house still looking like an ageing queen. But now there was an air of decay added to the overall impression. It was the window-boxes that did it. The flowers hadn't been attended and they had withered and died. They drooped over the edges of the boxes like the dried brown fingers of a long dead mummy. The coaching lamps hadn't been cleaned either, and the brass was dull and lifeless.

I walked past the house and knocked on the front door of its immediate neighbour. I worked my way up the street, then I started down the opposite side. Halfway down, I re-crossed the road and worked my way back up, finishing at the next door house on the opposite side. Out of the twenty houses I tried, I found seventeen people at home, and from fifteen of the seventeen, I learned nothing. The other two, while not exactly turning up trumps, at least meant that I hadn't wasted my time.

I called in at the pub at the end of the road, the one I had visited on the night it had all started. I greeted the barman like a long-lost friend, and he pretended to recognise me. Because he didn't, and felt that he should, he became more voluble than he would have been normally. His information, combined with what I had just learned, made the whole trip worthwhile.

Mrs. Jacoby lived in a building that was put up to celebrate the Crimean war, and should have been pulled down to celebrate the Boer War. She had a two-roomed apartment on the fourth floor, and she shared tap privileges with three other apartments on the same floor, the tap being located on the communal landing, next door to the toilet, which was also shared.

She answered the door to my knock, and over her head I could see into the apartment. There was a truculent looking youth in leather sitting at a bare wood table forking his dinner into his mouth. He didn't even look up as Mrs. Jacoby came out on to the landing quickly, and closed the door behind her. She started straight in on why she had fallen behind on the TV payments and it took me ten minutes to get across to her that I didn't come from the finance company, from the landlord, or from the police. But once she had got that fact firmly fixed in her head, she showed signs of becoming loquacious.

Yes, she had charred for poor Mr. Dunning, what took sick and died, two hours a day five days a week. Not Saturday or Sunday 'cos her Bob was at home and had to be fed. Having ascertained that fact, I told her to fetch her hat and coat and took her down to a handy pub and we really talked.

Horace was back on duty when I arrived home. No doubt he was wondering what had happened to Wallace. Between the two of them, they had made a complete balls of keeping me under surveillance. It wasn't really their fault, but I didn't imagine that Berat would be too pleased. He had struck me as a man who didn't make mistakes himself, and wouldn't tolerate them in others. Still, that was their problem. I had others of my own.

I poured myself a large drink, and read the evening paper. I washed up some dirty dishes and rinsed out a couple of pairs of socks. I washed a nylon shirt and hung it up to dry. I had another drink which I took with me to the bath. I trimmed my toenails, had a crap, read the evening paper again, and then had a shave. After that there seemed nothing left to do but to phone Berat's contact and tell him about the rendezvous.

I called the number he had given me and identified myself. Then I gave the time and the place. The message was repeated back to me by the person on the other end of the line, who then hung up. It was now seven thirty. I had twenty-six hours to wait. I broke all the rules and called Mary before eight o'clock. Fortunately, it was all clear, and after snarling at me gently for breaking the rules, she said she'd have dinner with me.

I got dressed and went out. I still hadn't picked up my stuff from the airport, which meant that I didn't have a topcoat. The evening was chilly, but I warmed myself up during the next twenty minutes while I was losing Horace. It is next to impossible for one man to tail another, if the one under surveillance knows that he is being followed. There are a thousand different ways to shake a tail, and I lost Horace round about number three. Having left him stranded on the down escalator at Sloane Square station, I called a taxi and gave the driver an address in Cheapside.

I am not a man who is normally disposed towards violence. I will walk ten miles to avoid trouble, and if trouble comes, I will try to talk my way out of it. As a last resort I will turn and run. But there comes a time when running is no good any more, for no other reason than that there is no longer any place to run to. Then all one can do is to turn and fight. The question then arises as to how one fights—clean or dirty. I'd learned very early in life that the man who fights clean winds up with his head in a sling, while the dirty fighter leaves the field of battle with nothing more painful than a troublesome conscience. That's always assuming he knows what a conscience is, which isn't usually the case.

The address I had given the taxi driver was Solly Weisman's. Solly runs a clock and watch repair shop just off Cheapside. At least, that's what he runs in the front of his place. What goes on in the back is anybody's guess. As far as I was concerned, what went on was a bit of judicious blackmail, so that I left the shop twenty minutes later with a gun.

Solly and I have known each other for years, and since leaving the Service. I have used him as my private armourer. My ability to do this is based on the fact that Solly deserted from the British army early in 1942, and, by a pure stroke of luck, I found out about it. The British army has a long memory, and even now, twenty-five years later, Solly could still be put away for a few years if they got their hands on him. So, while he hated me, if I asked for something hard enough, I got it.

What I asked for in this case was a Smith and Wesson .38 Police Special, and twenty-five rounds of ammunition. I don't like guns; I never have, but as a functional piece of equipment, they have their points. If I was going to be left alone with Berat for any length of time at all, I wanted to level the odds as much as possible. The gun, I felt, would help.

Solly tried to get me to take a holster as well, a soft chamois shoulder holster. This, in itself, was a sure sign that he hated me. A holster is strictly for the birds, or for those people who have no intention of using their gun. If a gun is going to be used, it should be tucked in the waistband of the trousers where it is easily accessible, and clearly visible. The sight of it by the opposition is often sufficient to obviate the necessity of using it. A gun in a holster is difficult to reach, and having reached it, difficult to get out. A man is liable to be dead three times over before he can clear a gun from a shoulder holster. Solly knew this, so he practically begged me to take one. I told him "no thank you" and promised to let him have the gun back in a couple of days. His soft brown eyes told me that he would be happy never to see the gun again, if it meant that I disappeared with it. I was his one link with the past, and while he was practically sure that I would never turn him in, the fact that I was in a position to do so offended his peace of mind.

Because of this, I checked every round of ammunition as soon as I got home, examining each round individually. Then I selected three cartridges at random and prised the lead from the cartridge case. I tipped out the powder in each case, and struck a lighted match to it. Each time it flared convincingly.

Then I wrapped the gun and the remaining ammunition in an old pair of pyjamas, and buried the bundle at the bottom of my dirty linen basket. Anyone adventurous enough to delve through *that* deserved to find something.

Then I brushed my teeth, took two Amplex, and went out to exercise my urges.

I took Mary to a small fish restaurant behind Eaton Square. There I stroked her thigh gently throughout dinner. She wanted to know where I had been and what I had been up to. But it was a polite curiosity rather than a genuine desire to know. Our relationship was so adjusted that any interest we had in each other was confined to those times we were together. Apart, we led completely individual lives with no strings and no comebacks. I watched her tucking into her food like there was no tomorrow and I wondered, as I often did, what the hell I was going to do when this girl got married. The thought crossed my mind, as it had the habit of doing, why didn't I marry her myself? I'd never asked her, and the reason was buried deep in my subconscious. Not deep enough however, that it didn't poke its murky little head up sometimes long enough for me to recognise it. I didn't ask her because I was frightened that she would say no. I am realistic enough to know that I am no catch yet, like a number of realists, I can fool myself quite adequately when I want to. As long as she didn't turn me down, I could bask in the fact that she might have said yes. So, I didn't ask her. I consoled myself with the fact that she *wasn't* married and at least while we were together this lovely, gentle, humorous creature was all mine. Dinner over, we went back to her flat and to bed.

I emerged into the early morning at three a.m. and drove home. I could see Horace a little way down the road, asleep in his car. I thought for a moment that I should go and waken him. At least he would know that I had come home. Then I thought the hell with him. I let myself in, made a cup of hot chocolate, and went to bed.

According to the label on the tin, deep undisturbed sleep should have followed. It didn't. I wrestled with my pillows for an hour; then I got up and made myself a strong, black coffee. I took it back to bed with me, and wide awake now, I did some top-grade thinking, mostly about Mrs. Jacoby.

She had warmed towards me after the second port and lemon, and although her speech had started to slur slightly, she had been very positive about what she had told me. She had arrived at Dunning's house the morning after the murder, unaware that anything had happened. She found the place full of large young men in lounge suits, the police long ago having been chased out by Max's staff. They had told her that Mr. Dunning had suffered a heart attack the previous evening. Then they had asked her to look around the house to see if she could spot whether or not anything was missing. She had done so, and reported that as far as she was concerned everything was where it should be. They had thanked her politely and driven her home. Unfortunately, or fortunately, depending on whose point of view one took, she had forgotten her handbag. So later that evening, after she had fed her Neanderthal son, she had gone back to the house to fetch it. The Service men had gone and she had let herself in with her own key, which for some extraordinary reason she wore on a piece of string around her neck. She knew where she had left her handbag and she went straight to it in the upstairs bathroom.

Then, as she put it, she "'ad the shock of 'er life". The bedroom was full of women's clothes. There were dresses hanging in the wardrobe, and the drawers were full of sweaters, blouses and underwear. The dressing table held perfumery and other such female accoutrements, the like of which she had never seen in Dunning's house before.

"I thought for a moment as 'ow I'd come into the wrong 'ouse," she said. "But I knew I 'adn't, so I thought as 'ow the 'ouse had been sold to someone else already, and poor Mr. Dunning not even in his grave yet. So I just grabbed me 'andbag and left quick afore anyone 'cused me of trespassin'."

She had a spot of bother with the word "trespassing" but I was well satisfied by now. I bought her two more port and lemons and left her in the Snuggery with a group of her cronies who had been eyeing us for the last hour dying to know what it was all about. They weren't the only ones. I was pretty desperate to know what it was all about myself.

I made myself another coffee, took it back to bed, and went all over it again. But, whichever way I tried to work it out, it always led back to Danielle. And Danielle wasn't going to give away one little thing, not to me anyway.

Then, about five thirty, I started to get a nasty idea. It was buried deep in the back of my skull and it took me more than an hour to ferret it out. When I finally made it, and spread it out in the cold dawn light, it didn't look as feasible as I had first thought. It still looked nasty, but much too nasty to take really seriously. But Max was the prime mover, so I took it seriously.

Finally, at seven a.m. I dropped off to sleep. My alarm was set for eight, so waking up was like returning from the dead. I staggered around the flat like a man suffering from shell shock, dragging myself awake in easy stages between coffee, bathroom and three cigarettes which tasted like dirty blotting paper and set me coughing like an advanced tubercular case. By nine thirty, I judged myself fit to communicate with my fellow creatures. I telephoned Miss Roberts and told her I wouldn't be in. Then I unwrapped the gun from its hiding place, and nearly ruptured myself trying to tuck it in the waistband of my trousers. I began to wish I had listened to Solly and accepted the offer of a holster. I put all the ammunition loose in my jacket pocket and left the apartment.

I got into my car and after giving Horace plenty of time to manoeuvre his car out, and start to follow me, I drove to London Airport. I parked the car and went into Number Two Building. I walked up the stairs, where I joined a stream of passengers going through to Customs and Immigration, bound eventually for

Majorca. I caught a glimpse of Horace's face as he watched me leave. His mouth was hanging open. Then, as he dashed for the nearest telephone, I walked over to a customs officer and showed him the note I had received reporting the arrival of my luggage from France. He told me that I could pick it up in the bonded warehouse that dealt with freight. I thanked him and remarked on the weather and how fortunate people were to be going away to the sun this time of the year. He agreed with me, and said how some people have all the luck, and how he couldn't afford to go abroad even if he did have the time, which he didn't. With embellishments, this took up ten minutes, so by the time I walked out again, Horace was long gone. I hoped that Berat wouldn't take the report that I had left the country too seriously.

I picked up my suitcase and my overcoat, signed a couple of forms and returned to my car. Just to be on the safe side, I peered under the bonnet before I got in. I wouldn't have put it past Horace to have exceeded his duties somewhat, and prepared a surprise for me. But there was nothing under there that wasn't supposed to be, and wrapped in cashmere, I piloted my way out of the airport and pointed the car towards Box Hill. My early morning flights of fancy were far too wild to accept without a second opinion, and Gunther's was the only opinion, apart from my own, that I could trust.

He pretended indifference when I arrived, and I let him sweat at it for a while. Finally, he could wait no longer.

"So tell me!" he said.

I told him, right from the time I had last seen him just before I left for France. I didn't realise how much there was to tell until I laid it all out on the line like that, and it took me more than an hour. He didn't interrupt me once and, when his daughter appeared with lunch, he merely snarled at her to serve it quickly and get out.

"That's about it," I said finally, sitting back. He didn't say anything for a couple of minutes and I let the silence rest between us.

Then he asked a couple of questions. They were questions of fact, not theory, and I answered them as accurately as I could. There was another silence, which lengthened to six minutes before he spoke again.

"You have drawn conclusions?" he asked.

"Plenty," I said.

"So let's have them," he said impatiently.

"The first one is a little far out," I said. "But it could fit, if you've got a strong stomach."

I gave him the nasty idea I had conceived at five thirty that morning. Here, with the birds racketing and the sun shining, it seemed even further out than I had at first visualised. Halfway through I started to say so, but he dragged me back on the rails and made me finish.

"It fits," he said at last.

"Like a tailor-made coffin," I said. "But even Max wouldn't dream up a scheme like that."

Gunther didn't say anything. He just looked at me, and finally I nodded my head.

"Yes, he would," I agreed.

"But that is only one story, one set of conclusions. Let us examine some others," he suggested.

But each one we examined had holes in it large enough to drive a bus through and we found ourselves coming back to the first idea time and time again. It was the only theory that fitted all the circumstances.

"It's sick," I said.

"It's a sick world," said Gunther.

I agreed. It was a sick world, and nowhere was it sicker than in the grey half-world which was ruled by Max and men like him. I had opted out of it once before, and now here I was again, in so deep that I needed a sludge dredger to get me out. This time there was no pretty young girl with blood where her face should have been, but there was a trail of dead and dying bodies stretching back to the beginning. There was Dunning and Alworthy and there were the two Service men on the autoroute. There was also the fifteen names in the notebook who were as good as dead, and there was yours truly who was still walking around on two legs, but who might as well be in a coffin six feet down as far as the overall plan was concerned.

I thanked Gunther for his time, and for once I wasn't embarrassed when he kissed me goodbye. He, better than anyone else, knew that if we were correct in our diagnosis, I stood about as much chance of getting clear of the set-up as Max getting religion. Something of Gunther's grimness must have transmitted itself to his daughter because she gave me the first kind look I had ever received from her. She even unbent sufficiently to wish me luck as she showed me out.

I drove back to London and parked in a no waiting area while I went down to pick up the notebook. The toilet where I had hidden the key was occupied and I hung around for a few minutes while the attendant eyed me mournfully. He was just working up enough enthusiasm to start getting awkward, when the toilet was vacated, and I slipped in and slammed the door behind me.

For one moment I thought they must have had the plumbers in and the key was gone. I fished around desperately, elbow deep in the cistern, and then I found it lodged in the most inaccessible corner.

Up in the concourse, I opened the left luggage locker and extracted the notebook. Then, feeling that everyone in the place had eyes only for me, I walked up to street level and went back to my car. There was no policeman hovering around the car and no parking ticket taped to the windscreen, the first bit of luck I'd had since the whole mess started.

Just before I drove out of London, I thought about calling Mary. But there didn't seem much point. There was nothing I could say to her except good-bye, and I hate good-byes.

I stopped for a few minutes in a lay-by about twenty minutes out of London. There I loaded the gun, and did one other little job. Then I restarted the car and pointed it towards the rendezvous Max had chosen with such loving care.

Twenty-five miles east and slightly south of London, you are slap in the middle of Kent. It's beer growing and farming country, dotted with oast houses and tidy, prosperous farms. The Garden of England it's called, and in some circumstances, I suppose I could have enjoyed a leisurely drive along country roads lined with neat hedges that marked out fields full of cows and sheep and other agricultural impedimenta. But this wasn't the circumstance. To me the cows looked bovine and stupid, and the sheep reminded me too much of my own predicament for comfort—that of an innocent being fattened for the not-too-distant slaughter. But there was an edge I had over my wool-bearing compatriots—I *knew* I was being led to the chopping block and I had enough meanness in me to work on some form of protest.

In the centre of a triangle formed by Wrotham, West Malling and Aylesford, there is an airfield. Or rather there *was* an airfield. It formed part of the Greater London defence system during the war. After the war, when the Americans had left and the shouting had died down, an enterprising local tycoon had started a flying club there and promptly gone broke. Since then, the huts that had once provided billets and administration buildings for upwards of twelve hundred men had been used successively by squatters and itinerant hop pickers down from London. More recently, they had been used as cow sheds, but as there was no one willing to spend any money on their upkeep, they had become so dilapidated that even the cows wouldn't use them any longer and they had started to collapse gently, one by one. In the centre of the airfield was the only building that could lay any claim to having withstood the ravages of time. This had been the control tower and, although the operational section of it had long ago been stripped of all its trappings, there were still four concrete walls and a roof.

This, then, was the infallible rendezvous picked by Max as a place where his men of the Heavy Squad would be able to pick up Berat the moment the transfer had been made. There were twenty-five different ways of approaching the place and, naturally enough, twenty-five different ways of leaving it. To be sure of picking up Berat, Max would have needed to call out the entire Brigade of Guards. The reluctant conclusion I had been forced to was that Max didn't want to pick up Berat at all. But this was reasoning that, while fitting all the known facts, still remained within the area of speculation. And because I could no longer afford to speculate, I arrived at the airfield a full two and a half hours before the appointed rendezvous time.

I drove round the perimeter once, then turned off on to a side lane and parked my car half a mile away, well off the road. Then I walked back the way I had come. I reached the edge of the airfield at five p.m., still two hours before time and, feeling rather foolish, I selected a tree and climbed it.

I suffered a scraped knee, a bruised elbow and a severe attack of vertigo before I was satisfied that I had clambered high enough. Resting uncomfortably in a junction of trunk and branches, I looked around. I could see the whole of the airfield, right round the perimeter to the cluster of collapsed walls that had been the administration centre. The control tower stood alone and phallic in the middle of the airfield about seven hundred yards from where I was. It was a fine, clear evening and, with the binoculars I had brought along, I could pick out detail with absolute clarity. After ten minutes, I had satisfied myself that I was the only person anywhere near the airfield. It was so bloody quiet and peaceful that it wouldn't have taken much effort to convince myself that I was the only person for five hundred miles, but the idea was so tantalising that I banished it severely.

After half an hour, I realised that if I didn't come down from the tree soon, I was going to do irreparable damage to my spine, which was jammed against the main trunk, and my crotch, which was wrapped around a particularly knotty branch. Moving about just made it worse, so I started to tuck the binoculars back in their case, when suddenly my aches and pains were forgotten. There was a car moving slowly around the perimeter road. Using the binoculars again, I could see that there were at least four occupants. One of them could have been Max, but it was impossible to tell for certain.

I followed the car as it made a complete circuit of the airfield, passing almost beneath me. Then, as it reached the far huts once more, I lost it for a moment behind the walls. When it reappeared, it was minus two of its passengers. It figured—two detachments from the Heavy Squad, two men in each. One detachment had been dropped off at the far side of the airfield, and it was reasonable to assume that the other pair would station themselves somewhere near where I was perched. But the Heavy Squad didn't interest me at this moment. It was Max I wanted to see.

I didn't doubt that he would be lurking around somewhere nearby. He enjoyed field work, as long as it wasn't too dangerous, and providing it was somewhere in the British Isles. He used to say he liked to get out to see how "his boys" operated. But he would no more have left the country than he would have taken up knitting. Somewhere deep in his shifty mind there was the fear that, should he leave the protection of these shores, he would be spirited away to some Red dungeon, there to suffer torture, brainwashing and worse. He was probably right. The number of people who would have liked to get their hands on Max was formidable.

The car stopped three hundred yards away from my perch, but the two occupants didn't get out. They were still ninety minutes early for the rendezvous and they weren't going to get off their arses until it was absolutely necessary. But they had chosen their parking spot well. Although I could see both them and the control tower, it would be impossible for anyone in the control tower to see the car, due to half a dozen strategically placed trees. If Berat followed his instructions carefully, he would turn off the road on to the airfield perimeter just to the left of the huts and drive straight to the tower. He'd never see the waiting car, and it was safe to assume that the two men who had been dropped off near the huts would remain well under cover.

So far everything seemed above board, as long as you were willing to discount the actual site. Max had said he would have Heavy Squad ready to pick up or pick off Berat after our little transaction, and here they were. If I'd had a less suspicious mind, I'd have accepted the whole thing at face value and proceeded as planned. But I had no intention of proceeding anywhere until I had located Max.

And locate him I did. Ten minutes after the first car stopped, away on my left, I picked up another car as it meandered round the perimeter. There was only one occupant, the driver, and halfway round the airfield I identified him through the binoculars. As though to confirm my identification, I saw him take a hand off the wheel and mop his eyes with a handkerchief. If he thought his eyes were giving him trouble now, just wait until I was through with him. I started to clamber down to the ground.

I ripped my jacket halfway down, and I silently thanked the powers that I had left my new overcoat in the car. By the time I dropped to the ground, Max's car must have passed the one with the waiting Heavy Squad, and I cut through the bushes and out on to the perimeter just in time for Max to see me and stick on the brakes.

He didn't get out of the car, but at least he had the courtesy to wind down the window.

"You're early," he said.

I leaned on the side of the car looking down at him.

"So are you," I said.

"Checking the disposition of the troops."

"How many men?" I asked.

"A dozen," he said. I let it go.

"Any changes in the plan?"

He shook his head.

"After the transaction, you get him to leave first. Give him five minutes. We will have picked him up by then. You can come out safely after that and I'll meet you here."

"How do we know he'll come alone?"

"He probably won't," said Max. "But while you're doing your bit of business, we'll wrap up whoever he's brought along. Simple."

I decided the only simple thing about the whole bit was me for letting it go so far—and Max for thinking I'd let it go any further.

"I spoke to Danielle today," I said.

He covered up very well.

"Danielle?" he repeated. His eyes had started to water again.

"You remember Danielle," I said. "I used to be married to her."

"That's right," he said. "I remember now."

He pinned a very convincing look on his face which was meant to convey polite curiosity at my mentioning something that couldn't possibly have any bearing on the issue at hand.

"She was married to Dunning too," I said.

"Yes?" He had decided to humour me.

"Until two years ago," I said.

He decided he had had enough.

"That's all very fascinating," he said. "But this is hardly the time or the place to discuss your domestic failures."

"How did you get to her?" I persisted.

"To whom?"

I didn't even bother to answer. There was a long pause while he thought about this latest development and the repercussions it could have. Then he decided to ignore the whole thing. He started the engine.

"I'll meet you afterwards," he said.

I had to hand it to him. Even at this stage he was prepared to bluff it out. He stopped bluffing when I poked the gun across the edge of the door. I let him get a good long look at it, and the little lead snouts poking at him from the chambers.

"Switch it off," I said. He switched off and started to play it cool.

"You haven't got a licence for that."

"Sue me," I said.

"Put it away, John," he said affably. "Let's talk."

"So talk." I didn't move the gun.

"You know this area is swarming with Heavy Squad."

"Four men don't swarm," I said. "Especially when two of them are nearly a mile away."

He looked from my face to the gun and back to me again.

"You're getting yourself into trouble," he said. He had started to look mean.

"I'm already in trouble," I said. "This is getting cut."

"With a gun?"

"If it helps."

"What trouble are you in?" he said. It was an old habit of his. You started off by asking the questions and two minutes later he was asking them and you were so busy defending yourself you didn't have time to remember what it was you started out to discover.

"You tell me," I said.

He started to look innocent until I jabbed the gun into his throat, just below his right ear.

"Tell me about Danielle," I said.

He thought it over for a moment. Then he decided that I was a *schmook* and he might as well tell me anyway.

"Would you have come in if I'd asked you?" he said.

"No."

"That's what I thought. I wanted you in. She seemed as good a way as any."

"You paid her?"

He shrugged.

"A couple of hundred pounds." Danielle would have sold her own mother for fifty; Max had got no bargain.

"And Dunning?" I asked him.

"He had the names. We had to get them from him before the Chinese did."

"Why didn't you just move in and take them?"

This one worried him for a moment, but only a moment.

"We didn't know where the notebook was," he said. "Dunning could have hidden it anywhere. It was important enough for him to keep quiet about it, whatever form of persuasion we used."

From what I could remember of Dunning, he had seemed the sort that would have wanted an anaesthetic to have his toenails cut.

"You're lying Max," I said.

He started to look indignant, then he changed his mind.

"So, I'm lying," he said.

"Why did you think I could find the notebook if you couldn't?"

"You found it."

"Because I was supposed to. Danielle told you about the hiding place."

"You're talking nonsense," he said.

"I haven't started yet." I gave him a little jab with the gun, just below the ear. "Now you listen to me, Max. When I go wrong you can tell me. Until then keep your big fat mouth shut, or I'll take your ear off." He started to reach in his inside pocket and I jabbed him again.

"My eye drops," he said.

I nodded and watched him extract his eyedrops and perform the necessary.

"Ready?" I said finally. He nodded.

"This is the way I read it," I said. "I was *meant* to find the notebook and the whole business about my involvement with the Dunning killing and Inspector Diaman was designed to look good to the other side, to Berat. I had something which you wanted badly enough to get me off a murder charge and pay me fifty thousand pounds for. Therefore, says Berat, it must be pretty bloody important. You rig a convincing handover in France, put up the money for the notebook, then you blow the rendezvous. It didn't matter a toss to you that you were sending two of your own men to the chop. All you wanted was Berat to get the notebook there and then. But that's where your scheme fell flat on its arse. There were only two dead men instead of three, me being the third. You must have been choked. Two men dead, fifty thousand quid out of pocket, and nothing to show for it. It couldn't have looked very good upstairs. So you devise a salvage operation— and if you tell me you're going to pick up Berat after he gets the notebook, then I shall tell you that you're a bloody liar. He *gets* the notebook, he has always been going to get it. Your only problem was to make sure that it didn't look like the plant that it is. Which raises the question, what's in the notebook?"

"Names," said Max.

"I know that. Whose names?"

"Agents," he said.

"Whose?"

"Russian," said Max. And the whole thing fell into place. Berat would get the names believing they were those of Western agents, and the Chinese would act accordingly. Doors would be broken down in the middle of the night, and fifteen people would be driven away in fast motor cars, or rickshaws, or whatever they use in the People's Republic. There would be no trials, just fifteen empty places where once there had been people.

The Russians would be unable to scream because the agents shouldn't have been there in the first place. But the cold front between the two countries would widen considerably, and that could do the West nothing but good. But it had to have been made to look genuine. If Berat or his employers suspected that the names were Russian and not Western agents, then the two big enemies would come closer together, united against the common foe.

It was a fine scheme until one started to count the dead bodies that Max had strewn along the wayside. I think about here he expected me to congratulate him. He had started to look a little smug.

"Who got the names in the first place?" I asked him.

"Dunning. He was on a mission to Moscow. One of our people over there contacted him."

"Why did he wind up with a cut throat?"

"Alworthy was a Russian agent. They found out about the leak and tried to plug it."

"By killing him?" I said.

"Alworthy knew we were on to him. He got impatient."

"Dunning was above board," I said.

"Completely," said Max. "He brought us the names as soon as he came back from Moscow. That's when I took over."

The little bastard was proud of himself. I felt like shooting him there and then, and hang the consequences. But I resisted the temptation.

"What's supposed to happen now?"

"Berat gets the notebook, you get paid, and I get my fifty thousand pounds back," said Max.

"And the names in the book?"

He shrugged.

"Occupational hazard," he said. He didn't feel any justification was needed, but in case I wanted one, he threw it to me casually. "Anyway, they're Russian agents."

I suppose I'd been too long out of the Service, because it didn't help much. When I spoke again it was slowly. I wanted him to get the full benefit of what I was saying.

"Max," I said. "You can go and stuff yourself." I didn't use that particular verb, but the meaning was the same.

He looked at me blankly. He honestly didn't understand what I was getting at.

"It all ends here," I said. "I don't meet Berat, and I take the notebook away and burn it."

This got to him where it hurt. He could see the whole torturous business going out of the window. What really upset him was the thought of the eventual post mortem, where he would have to account for two dead agents and a petty cash voucher for fifty thousand pounds. That was on the debit side and he would have nothing with which to balance the book.

"You can't do that," he said.

"Don't take any bets on it," I told him. But I wasn't feeling as confident as I sounded. He was taking the news badly, but not nearly as badly as he should have been.

"You've got no choice," he said.

"Prove it to me."

"If you don't turn up, Berat will go after you, and in case he has any difficulty, I shall give him a hand. It's a small world, John, not nearly big enough for you to hide in, especially as you're broke."

All too true I decided. Then he helped me on my way.

"On the other hand," he said. "You do everything as planned and you wind up with half of twenty-five thousand pounds and nobody chasing you."

"What about Berat when he finds out I've sold him a plant?" I asked.

"He's a professional," said Max.

He had a point there. If a deal went sour, that was that. The professional would write it off and get on with the next. Revenge was for the birds.

Max could see he was getting to me, so he pursued his advantage in the area where it would do the most good.

"You must be way out of pocket by now," he said. "I checked—and you were on your uppers before you started. So to add to your problems, if you don't go through with it, you'll probably wind up inside for debt."

I was weakening fast and he knew it.

"So be a good fellow," he said. "Take that gun out of my ear and I'll forget I ever saw it."

I took the gun out of his ear. There didn't seem to be anything else I could do. He leaned forward and restarted the engine.

"Don't forget," he said. "Give him five minutes before you come out."

"So's you can wrap him up," I said.

He grinned at me, a nasty little grin.

"So's he can get well clear," he said. "I'll wait for you here."

I tucked the gun back into my trousers.

"All right, Max," I said.

He continued to grin at me as he drove away. If anything, the grin was nastier than it had started out, and suddenly I felt cold.

I walked back to the car and fetched my overcoat. Still cold, I walked back to the airfield and, avoiding the car with the Heavy Squad, I carried on to the control tower.

It was nearly dark when I reached it. Before going in, I looked around the silent airfield, feeling the three sets of eyes that were no doubt watching me. I felt like giving them a stiff two fingers, but as a gesture of defiance it would have fallen as flat as I felt, so I just turned and went into the control tower instead.

There was nothing much left of it except the four walls and the roof. There was a dilapidated concrete staircase leading up through a hole in the roof. This had once provided access to the first floor, but as the first floor had been constructed entirely of wood and glass, it had long since gone. All the staircase now provided was somewhere for me to sit while I waited for Berat.

Before settling down, however, I removed the notebook from my hip pocket and hid it beneath a pile of rubble in the corner. I placed the gun on the sixth stair from the bottom, and covered it with a piece of sacking that had been used for God knows what. Then I sat down and waited.

While waiting I did some retrospective thinking. If my greed for one hundred and fifty pounds hadn't blinded me into taking the job Danielle had dangled in front of me; if I hadn't barged into Dunning's house like a drunken Irishman on St. Patrick's night; if I hadn't allowed myself to be conned by everyone and his mother; if I hadn't... I gave up. The trouble was, I *had*, and that's why I was here.

I tried occupying my time with dreams of what I could do with my share of the loot, but as I didn't really expect to lay my hands on it, it proved an abortive process.

I was still trying to think of other ways to occupy my time when Berat arrived. He appeared suddenly in the doorway and frightened me to death. I had been expecting him to arrive by car, and his sudden, silent appearance, put ten years on to my life. He looked the same as he had at the château, immaculate and just as incongruously out of place. His eyes flicked once round the inside of the control tower, then back to me and he smiled.

"You're punctual," he said.

"I didn't have so far to come as you did," I told him.

"The journey was well worth it," he said. Then when I didn't move, he added a codicil. "Wasn't it?"

It wasn't that I was feeling rebellious again; it was just that suddenly I felt a hundred years old and he could have shoved a stick of dynamite up my backside and I wouldn't have been able to find the energy to pull it out. He stepped further into the building.

"Are you all right?" he asked.

There was concern in his voice and I wondered how soft his shoulder would be for crying on. But then I pulled myself together. His concern was for the notebook, not for my peace of mind.

"I'm sorry," I said. "I'm getting old."

"Old and rich," he said.

He stepped out of the door and reappeared a moment later with a briefcase. I wondered whether he had picked it up or had it handed to him. Then I decided that I didn't much care. I nodded towards the stairs.

"I'd like to see it," I said.

"Of course," he said.

He moved over to the stairs, and opening up the briefcase, he up-ended it. It was a grandiloquent gesture, but a little impractical, as everything tumbled out every which-way. Two hundred and ten thousand dollars in negotiable currency is a lot of paper. It spilled from the third stair, on to the second and the first, covering all three stairs with impressive ease. It was lucky there wasn't a wind blowing or we'd have lost the lot. As it was, a gentle evening breeze caressed the edges of some of the notes, causing them to rustle with hynoptic effect.

I stepped towards the loot, but he held up his hand suddenly.

"Please," he protested.

He was right of course. I fetched the notebook from where I had hidden it and pitched it to him. He caught it neatly and backed away from the money. I watched him as he flipped it open on page one. He checked the contents of page one quickly, and satisfied, he riffled through half a dozen pages and checked another entry. If he looked at the last page, I was dead. I measured the distance between me and the place where I had hidden my gun, and tried to coax some energy into my tired old legs. But it wasn't necessary. He looked up at me and smiled.

"That all seems to be in order," he said. He nodded towards the money.

"You're satisfied?"

I walked over to the money, and picking out a couple of notes I ran a quick check on them.

"Satisfied," I said.

He turned to go. Then, at the door, he turned back again.

"You worried me at first," he said. "I didn't like the way you kept losing the tail I provided."

"It wasn't hard," I said. He smiled.

"Perhaps not, but I couldn't see why you considered it necessary."

I shrugged.

"Old habits die hard," I said. He waved his arm, embracing the surroundings.

"Then this," he said. "When I heard about it, I thought the whole thing was beginning to become too melodramatic to be genuine. I nearly didn't come."

"But you did," I said.

"Yes, I did." He held the notebook up. "One way or another, I had to get hold of this. I expected a trap, but I came anyway."

"Expecting a trap, you must have come prepared," I said. He produced a gun suddenly. Or, rather, a gun suddenly appeared in his hand. I had a vague glimpse of a holster, low beneath his arm, before his jacket flapped back. So much for my theory on holsters. He held the gun loosely but efficiently. There was no threat implied.

"I'm impressed," I said. I was, too.

"It wasn't meant to impress," he said.

"I know. That makes it even more impressive. Personally, I don't like guns."

"Then I suggest you leave yours buried under that rubble when you leave," he said with a grin.

"*Touché,*" I said. "But I still don't like them."

"Nor do I," he said. "But they do have their uses."

He looked at me steadily for a moment. Then he reholstered his gun. It disappeared almost as quickly as it had appeared. For a man who didn't like guns, he handled one remarkably well.

"It's a pity you're going out of business," he said. "We could have done some work together in the future."

"Would you continue in business with this?" I indicated the money.

"Yes, I would," he said. "I enjoy it."

I started to go off him round about here. Anyone who enjoyed doing the work that he did must have had something seriously wrong with him somewhere.

"Perhaps we'll meet again," he said.

"I doubt it."

He smiled again and then went out of the door. I checked my watch and started to gather up the money, stuffing it back into the briefcase. Berat might have had a dozen men out there with him, but I couldn't even be bothered to find out. As far as I was concerned, our dealings were over and if I never saw him again, it would be too soon.

I repacked the briefcase in three minutes. I collected my gun and blew the cement dust out of the barrel. I tucked it back in my trousers and checked my watch once again. The five minutes were up and I started out to meet Max.

Just as I reached the door, I heard a shout from away on my left.

"Smith!"

I turned towards the voice and caught my foot on a chunk of cement and stumbled. Because of this the bullet missed me, chopping a chunk of concrete from the outside wall just where my head had been a second before. Instead of regaining my balance after tripping, I followed through and went flat on my face. The second bullet would have castrated me if I hadn't hit the deck. And there I lay, my nose buried in mud, petrified with fear, and so angry I could have eaten nails.

That elegant, double-crossing Albanian bastard, with his beautiful suits and his silk shirts! Next time he flashed his pearly choppers at me, I'd knock them through the back of his head.

Then I realised that, unless I got my arse off the ground pretty soon, there wouldn't be a next time. It was pretty dark, so they must have been using some form of infrared sight. I wondered for a moment whether Max would call up the Heavy Squad to get me out of trouble. But the idea was so ludicrous, it only served to remind me how scared I really was.

I fumbled beneath me trying to pull my gun out, but due to my fall, it had slipped below my waistband and was now flopping around inside my trousers. I couldn't remember whether I'd put the safety catch on, and I spent a frantic minute groping inside my trousers wondering whether I'd accidently snag the trigger and blow my own balls off.

I extracted it finally, still face down in the mud and tried to work out what I was going to do with it. As long as I lay where I was, I was obviously all right. If they had still been able to draw a bead on me, I would be dead by now. The trouble was I couldn't work out from where they were shooting, so I didn't know whether to wriggle backwards, forwards or sideways. I settled for backwards. At least the walls of the control tower would offer some form of protection.

I ripped my overcoat to shreds in the next few minutes, and if I'd been angry before, now I was livid. Once through the door, I wriggled sideways and then clambered to my feet. There was a hole in the far wall which had once been a window, so I kept well clear of it. I had no idea how many men Berat had with him and, knowing him as I did, he was probably covering all exits.

My immediate panic began to abate somewhat. I was still frightened, but no longer petrified. This was probably due to the fact that I was now perpendicular instead of horizontal. I knew I wasn't as frightened as before because now I started to try to analyse a way out of the mess. First, I couldn't go out of the door. Whoever he was, he wouldn't miss next time. Second, I couldn't go out of the window, because that was obviously covered as well. Third, I couldn't stay where I was; there was no future in it.

So I went on to the roof. I was clambering through the hole at the top of the staircase before I realised that I was still clutching the briefcase. In fact I'd never let go of it, even when I had fallen flat on my face, and afterwards when I was groping one-handed for my gun. I'd been half an inch off dying and I had clung to the money like it really mattered. I decided that I was an avaricious bastard and left it at that.

Climbing on to the roof meant that I had to stick my head through the hole first. This I did in easy stages, bobbing up for a split second the first time, slightly longer the second, longer still for the third. Finally, I managed to hold it up there for a full five seconds before my nervous reflexes jerked it down again. But behaving like an irrational jack-in-the-box wasn't going to achieve anything, so stamping firmly on my screaming nerves, I stuck my head up once more, and kept it there. The top of my skull remained where it was and a minute later I wriggled out on to the exposed flatness of the roof, dragging the briefcase behind me. There was a foot high parapet around the edge of the roof which effectively screened me from anyone at ground level, and I just prayed that Berat's men hadn't taken to tree climbing like I had done. But nobody shot at me again, so I made myself as comfortable as possible, and began to wait.

The hunted has an advantage over the hunter inasmuch as he can go to ground and then wait for the hunter to come for him. Whereas the hunter, with orders to kill, must continue to advance until he is satisfied that his task has been successfully completed.

They waited an hour before they moved in. When they did, it was quietly and efficiently. Wherever Berat had got these men, it wasn't from the same stable as Horace and Wallace. I was reluctantly forced to the conclusion that Berat himself would be long gone by now. The notebook was too valuable to risk in deeds of idle assassination.

There was a small scuff of sound from the front of the tower, and a similar sound from the back. They had approached from two directions simultaneously. I edged myself forward so that my head was inches away from the stairwell. A moment later I heard another sound as a man climbed in through the window. There was a pause, then he spoke to his companion who had obviously reached the door.

"He's gone," said a voice.

There was another pause, then a flashlight clicked on. The light leaked up through the stairwell, inches from my nose.

"Look on the roof," said another voice. He was the bright one.

A sudden shaft of light streamed up through the stairwell. I backed away quickly to the edge of the roof, and for the first time I let go of the briefcase. I left it on the roof, while I lowered myself over the edge and dropped to the ground. To me it sounded like a bag of coals dropped forty feet onto corrugated iron, but then I'm sensitive. The two men in the control tower didn't hear a thing, probably because the one on his way up to the roof was concentrating on not getting his head blown off, while the other one was blundering around in the dark.

I edged my way along the outside wall until I was level with the window. I drew my gun carefully and checked that the safety catch was off with my finger. Then I offered a silent prayer that Solly hadn't filed away the firing pin, because I was going to have to use the bloody thing in about ten seconds.

"He was up here," said the voice from the roof. "He's left the briefcase."

The one inside uttered an exclamation I assumed to be of satisfaction. I heard the footsteps on the roof as they crossed to the briefcase, then returned to the stairhead. Then as the footsteps started to descend, I risked a quick peek through the window. As it turned out there was no risk. One man was standing at the bottom of the stairs, looking up towards the other who was coming down. Just to make it easier for me, the one descending was shining his flashlight on to his companion.

I shot the one at the bottom first, and as the flashlight swung instinctively towards me, I shot at the light. He must have been holding it at waist level, because the bullet hit him in the stomach. The flashlight fell from his hand, bounced down the stairs, and finished on the ground, still switched on. The light that it gave was sufficient for me to see that the first man I had shot was as dead as he would ever be. The second was taking his time. He clutched his stomach, and stumbled down two more steps. Then he let go of the briefcase, and covered the last five stairs on his face.

An unholy silence suddenly clamped down, and I realised I was sweating like a pig, and my hand was shaking like I had the palsy. There was the stink of gunfire in the still night air and a lot of dust and smoke just beginning to settle.

At first, I was physically incapable of stepping back through the window, but after a moment the briefcase reasserted its old hypnotic effect and I scrambled through. I held the gun ready just in case, but my first diagnosis had been correct and both men were dead. I picked up the briefcase and then the flashlight. Out of curiosity, I flashed it on the faces of the two men. The first one didn't have much of a face left, my bullet having caught him just below his left eye. I didn't hold the flashlight on him longer than it took my stomach to heave. The second man was still clutching his stomach. His face wasn't pleasant by any means, but at least it was unmarked. It was an ordinary face as faces go, an anonymous everyday face, but the shock it gave me was twice that of the bloodied mask of his companion. The last time I had seen him had been through binoculars. He had been sitting with his partner in a car on the edge of the airfield, warming his bottom and waiting for the action to start.

No wonder Max hadn't felt it necessary to call out more than four of the Heavy Squad. He had assumed that four men were quite capable of taking care of little old me.

CHAPTER EIGHT

I RELOADED my gun, more to gain thinking time than for any other reason, then I sat down for a moment to try to work it all out. There had been four of the Heavy Squad, one pair on either side of the airfield. These two men had approached the control tower from opposite sides, so it was safe to assume that they comprised one from each pair. That meant there were still two men out there, one some place near the old huts and one near the parked car. As my own car lay in that direction, I decided to deal with the man near the car. Just how I was going to deal with him, I hadn't worked out, but by this time I was too angry to care. Berat pulling a double-cross had irked me enough, but Max doing it, that really choked me.

I gathered up the briefcase, picked up the flashlight and started out. It wasn't as dark as I had at first thought. There was a moon somewhere up there behind the clouds, and sufficient light leaked through to enable me not to have to use the flashlight all the time. But when I judged I was about two hundred yards from the car, I switched it on anyway. A man behind a torch is next to impossible to identify. I walked confidently, whistling a vague tuneless dirge between my teeth, for all the world like a man returning from a job well done. At least this was the impression I was trying to create, and it was successful. I'd nearly reached the car when a figure materialised behind it.

"O.K.?" he said.

I grunted an affirmative and walked closer. He came round to the front of the car, and the first he knew that all was not as it should be was when I showed him my gun.

To his credit, he didn't try anything stupid. His hands, which had been stuffed in his raincoat pockets, came out empty and he put them behind his head without having to be told.

"Into the car," I said.

He climbed into the car and I slammed the door behind him. I rested the gun across the top of the door, and still he didn't say a word.

"Take a message to Max for me," I said.

His eyes looked at mine. They were flat and expressionless. He was just a fellow doing a job and if the job had gone sour, it wasn't his fault.

"Tell him he can whistle for his money," I said. "And tell him not to hold his breath waiting for his grand scheme to pay off."

I withdrew the gun. The man was good, he knew the interview was at an end. He started the car and drove off without a word.

I waited until I judged he could no longer see me through the rearview mirror, then I bolted. By the time I reached my own car, I was practically useless. I threw the briefcase into the back and flopped into the driver's seat. I was puffing so hard I misted up the windscreen before I'd even started the engine. I followed the lane I was in for half a mile, then turned off on to a wider road. A mile further on I turned on to a minor road once more, all the time heading more or less south.

By three a.m. I was outside Lydd. I drove the car off the road into a small wood. Fifty yards into the trees I left it and walked back to the road. Then I waited two hours before I was able to hitch a ride to the airport.

There was a Geneva plane due out at seven thirty. I bought my ticket, and when the restaurant opened, I just had time for a substantial breakfast before catching the plane.

Two hours later I was in Geneva. I checked into the best hotel in the city, throwing Max's money around like a drunken sailor on Saturday night. From my suite, I called Gustave Holbecker. He agreed to meet me at the bank at one thirty.

During my days in the Service when I travelled Europe extensively, I had made Geneva my jumping off point both outwards and inwards. Returning to London after a job, I would invariably re-arrange my flight schedules so that I could stop over in Geneva, sometimes for a couple of days, sometimes only for a matter of hours. It became a habit and Max hated it. He couldn't understand why I did it and I never enlightened him.

If there is one thing that the Swiss treat with the respect that it deserves, it is money. To the Swiss, money is not something to be spent, but a commodity in its own right. It's the only place where money is not just a means to an end, but both the means and the end. And it is because of this that they make the arrangements that they do.

A safe deposit box in most countries is a place to store valuables so that the light-fingered fraternity can't get their hands on them. But should anything happen to the owner of the safe deposit, it is comparatively simple to obtain a court order whereby a responsible official can gain access to the deposit. I had £75,000-worth of Max's money, and there wasn't a single place in England where I could hide it. I owned safe deposit boxes in five different places at home, but knowing this, Max had only to exterminate me and set in motion the processes of law, and he would have had every one opened inside twenty-four hours.

But the Swiss don't go along with this at all. There you can rent safe deposits that can only be opened by the owner. And if the owner drops dead somewhere along the line, that safe deposit will remain closed until the crack of doom.

Needless to say, I owned one of these. In it, over my years in the service, I had deposited various documents and photographs that I considered necessary to insure my peaceful old age. After each job, I'd leave a small memento in Geneva, a little something that could effectively screw Max if he had come up with any bright ideas as to how important I was.

I hadn't been in Geneva for five years, but I knew that my box would still be there, untouched and inviolate. I also knew that only I, in person, could open it, and only then with the help of Gustave Holbecker. Because the Swiss are very careful. To obviate the possibility of anyone trying to impersonate a safe deposit owner, you can make it a rule at the bank that there must be two signatories for access to the deposit. One of them is the actual owner, the other is a local man of some standing, a lawyer, a doctor, or even a town councillor. Gustave was my man, a self-important little lawyer who had lived and worked in Geneva all his life. Unless he accompanied me to the bank, and identified me as being the man I said I was, I couldn't get into my deposit box even if the man in charge had been my own brother. For this small service I paid him a fee of £10 every time he came to the bank with me. He had about two hundred and fifty other clients for whom he performed the same service and, all in all, he probably made more money out of it than he did with his lawyering.

I waited for him outside the bank, clutching my briefcase like a mother with her firstborn. He bustled up to me through the lunchtime promenaders and looked at me shrewdly for a moment through rimless spectacles, while he sorted through his card index mind and identified me.

"Mr. Smith. It has been a long time," he said when he was satisfied that I was me.

"How are you, Gustave?" I said.

He spread his fat little hands.

"Business is not improving," he said. "But then neither is it deteriorating. And you?"

"So, so," I said, lying like a veteran.

"You wish access to your safe deposit?" he said.

I replied that I did and we went into the bank.

First we signed forms, then we waited while records were checked. They all knew Gustave as well as they knew their own families, but the whole rigmarole of identification was carried out as though he hadn't been near the place for ten years.

Finally, after much bowing and hand rubbing, we were escorted to the elevator. As an extra security measure, the elevators are constructed so that only one person at a time can get into them. I squeezed myself and my briefcase into this vertical coffin, and creaked downwards into the bowels of the earth. The door was opened at the bottom and I was greeted by another bank official who examined my pass and made me confirm that Gustave was in my party. Then the elevator was sent back up for Gustave, while we both stood there waiting. A minute later, Gustave joined us and the examination process was repeated.

Gustave and I were shown into a small room with a table and a couple of chairs. Two minutes later the bank official placed my safe deposit box in front of me. He bowed and walked out, and I heard the lock on the door click into place behind him. Gustave and I were now locked in the room and a "No Entry" sign was flashing outside the door. Until I rang the bell to be let out, Jesus Christ himself couldn't have come in.

There was a six number combination lock on the box and for one frightening moment I thought I had forgotten it. I spun the first four numbers, hesitated for a couple of seconds groping around in the past, and then it came to me. The lock clicked back and I opened the box. I would have liked to have spent a little time looking through the papers just to remind myself how much I hated Max, but it was a luxury I didn't really need to indulge in, so I let it ride. I opened the briefcase, and while Gustave stared fixedly at the opposite wall, his fat little face completely expressionless, I transferred the contents into the box. It was a tight squeeze, even after I'd taken out three thousand dollars for petty cash. But I managed, and I slammed the lid shut and spun the combination to relock it.

Then I pressed the bell and a bank official took the box away. As I watched it disappear from my sight, I felt like a mother must feel as she loses her only child.

We went up in the elevator one at a time, and upstairs I paid Gustave his fee. He shook me by the hand and puffed off to his next assignment. I settled the outstanding account for the safe deposit rental and paid up for the next ten years. I gave the briefcase to the doorman at the bank entrance and said I would pick it up later. Then I went shopping.

I'd arrived in Switzerland with the clothes that I stood up in, which included a badly torn cashmere overcoat. I went into Au Carneval de Venise in the Rue Montblanc, stripped down to the buff and bought half a dozen of everything from the skin outwards. I topped this sartorial binge with a new overcoat and, because I felt good, I made it vicuna this time. Then, feeling like Aristotle Onassis, I strolled back to my hotel. I hung a "Do not disturb" notice on the door and went to bed. I slept for eighteen hours straight.

It took Max three days to find me, which wasn't bad going, all things considered. Things had to come to the crunch eventually, and I didn't want to make it too difficult for the Service to locate me, so I spent most of those three days seated prominently outside a terrace restaurant on the main street.

In fact, I spotted them at the same time as they spotted me. I was enjoying my first bottle of Dom Perignon on the third morning, when I saw a small anonymous car pull up on the opposite side of the street. There was a hurried conversation between driver and passenger, then the passenger erupted from the car and dashed off to find the nearest telephone. The driver unfolded a newspaper and disappeared behind it.

I finished my champagne and paid the bill. I over-tipped outrageously and strolled back to the hotel slowly, so as not to make it too difficult for them. The Geneva office had never been too bright and I didn't imagine much would have changed in five years.

I settled my hotel bill before going upstairs to my room. There I packed and five minutes later when they exploded into my room, bristling with muscle, I was waiting for them. I believe they were sorry that I was so amenable. It had been a long, quiet year in Switzerland and they hadn't leaned on anyone for quite a time.

I was driven to the airport sandwiched between two men of the Swiss office. There I was handed over to two of the London men. They were a little nervous in case I started to scream that I was being kidnapped, so they stuck very close and didn't really relax until we were airborne. On the plane there didn't seem much point in trying to start a conversation, so I sat quietly for the hour and a bit to London.

Max pulled strings with immigration and customs and I was escorted into a car, straight off the plane. My suitcase came with me. Max wasn't going to have any customs officer rummaging through *that*.

We drove straight to the Farm. It's a place thirty miles out of London which the Service has owned for more years than I can remember. I believe things do get grown there, and there are certainly cows and suchlike wandering around. But the real business goes on in the farmhouse itself and, whatever it is, it's not agricultural. The Farm exists as a place to hide people, as a place to keep people, and sometimes as a place to kill people.

I was shown straight into the interrogation room, a tiled room with a drain let into the centre of the floor, containing a table and two chairs. Max was sitting behind the table, while beside him stood an anonymous looking member of the Heavy Squad. I didn't see the one behind the door, but I knew he was there. The point was emphasised a moment later when I felt a cold ring of steel pressed into the base of my skull. But I was giving nobody any arguments. I stood perfectly still and allowed the ball to stay in their court.

"Sit down," said Max.

The man standing beside Max moved round the table and dragged the chair into position for me. The one with the gun eased me into it.

"I'm going to kill you," said Max.

"Again?" I queried.

He ignored this.

"Before I do, though, I want some answers."

"I'll bet you do," I said.

"What was the meaning of the message you sent me?"

"About whistling for your money?"

"You said the plan wouldn't pay off. Why?"

"Because it won't."

"You told Berat?"

"No."

"Then why?"

So, I told him. I told him how I had started to smell out his plan and how I didn't like the stink. I described how I had stopped on my way down to the airfield and added a note of my own in the end of the notebook. It had been a simple note, one which I could have torn out before handing the book to Berat had I felt my suspicions were groundless. But they hadn't been, my interview with Max just prior to the rendezvous had proved that. Berat would have seen the note when he examined the book more carefully. It was a short note, four words only. I quoted them to Max verbatim.

"This is a plant," I said.

There was a long silence after this. Max sat there bidding a fond farewell to his grand design. Then he shrugged manfully and got to his feet.

"There's not much point in killing you then," he said.

I agreed.

"Give me the money and we'll call it quits," he said.

"No money," I said.

The room grew cold suddenly.

"The money," he said.

I shook my head again.

"My expenses have gone up," I said. "When I'm shot at by my own side and have to shoot people in return, then I come very high."

"How high?" said Max, knowing the answer.

"About seventy-five thousand pounds high," I said.

He looked at me steadily for a moment, his eyes as dry as dust. Then he nodded to the man standing behind me. For one blinding moment I thought I had overplayed my hand. Then I felt a quick, sharp jab low down on the side of my neck and, before I was able to climb to my feet, my mind slipped sideways and skidded off into the unknown.

When I came round it was purely a temporary arrangement. There was a large man in a white coat who I later learned was called Bruno. He asked me questions which I answered truthfully. With the stuff he pumped into me, I couldn't have done otherwise. I told him all about the safe deposit, and about the Swiss laws of access and about Gustave and about every other damn thing there was.

After these bouts of question and answer I was helped off to sleep again. Max's face appeared occasionally during these short periods of semi-consciousness, but that may only have been a hallucination.

My main hope now is that I can get out of this place before they yank my teeth. The ones I've got aren't anything to write home about, but at least they belong to me, and I prefer them to the National Health choppers which would be all I'd be able to afford on the outside.

Because whichever way you slice it, Max is going to have to get his money back. It's my only way out of this snake pit. The delicate piece of the operation comes in judging just how long I can keep him sweating before I throw in the towel. I'm rather proud of myself that I've hung on as long as I have, what with the food they give you here and Bruno's happy needle.

But other urges are starting to obtrude. I want to see Mary again before she forgets I exist. I want to drink a bottle of good wine, and I want to feel the sun on my back. Unimportant things in themselves perhaps, especially when balanced against the trouble Max must be having from upstairs, but they are beginning to weigh heavier in the scales. By the end of the week they'll probably be sufficient to swing the balance the other way. Then I shall have to tell Bruno to contact Max.

Max and I will have a little talk, and I will try to convince him to let me hang on to a couple of thousand quid to cover my expenses. He'll scream a little, but he'll have to wear it. Then will come a short, swift trip to Geneva, and that will be an end of it.

The trouble is, that after I have seen him and our financial transactions have been sorted out, he'll have his hooks deep enough into my hide to give him a pretty strong edge should he decide he wants me for anything in the future. If he starts waving my medical file around, I'm dead and buried. And with an edge like this, it doesn't take three guesses to know who Max will come to the next time he's got a particularly nasty job to be done. And knowing Max as I do, if he's got an edge, he'll use it like a hopped up axe fiend.

So perhaps I'll hang on longer than the end of the week. After all, I don't actually need my teeth to eat the muck they hand out here and the board and lodging is free. But if Bruno comes at me with that needle again, I'll shove it into him so far he'll need major surgery to get it out.

It's late now, and there's a fellow along the passage screaming like the maniac that he undoubtedly is. But the bed isn't uncomfortable and Bruno removed my strait-jacket half an hour ago. I think sleep is in order, and we'll review the whole situation again tomorrow.

ABOUT THE AUTHOR

Jimmy Sangster was an acclaimed screenwriter (*Curse of Frankenstein, Deadlier Than the Male, The Legacy,* etc), director (*Lust for a Vampire, Banacek,* etc), TV writer (*Wonder Woman, Cannon, BJ and The Bear, Kolchak,* etc) and novelist. His many books include *Touchfeather, Touchfeather Too, Blackball, Snowball, Hardball, The Spy Killer* and *Foreign Exchange.* He died in 2011.

A movie adaptation of *The Spy Killer,* written and produced by Sangster and directed by Roy Ward Baker, was released in 1969 and starred Robert Horton as John Smith, Sebastian Cabot as Max, and Jill St. John as Mary Harper.

Mystery 1608091
SANGSTER
2019

Made in the USA
Lexington, KY
08 September 2019